Shelter

a novel

ROBIN MERRILL

New Creation Publishing

New Creation Publishing
Madison, Maine

This novel is a work of fiction. Names, characters, businesses, organizations, places, events, and incidents are either the products of the author's imagination or used in a fictitious manner. Any resemblance to actual persons, living or dead, or actual events is purely coincidental.

Library of Congress Control Number: 2015943195

ISBN-13: 978-0-9912706-5-1
ISBN-10: 0991270657

For Lisa Berry

Chapter 1

She had no good reason to head toward Maine. Yet, when Maggie pulled out of her Massachusetts driveway, the steering wheel turned right. It just sort of happened, without her thinking too much about it.

True, she wanted to avoid crowds, and on some level, knew that she had a better chance at that if she turned north. True, she was a Stephen King junkie, so while she didn't consciously *choose* to turn toward the mastermind of horror, her subconscious may have felt the call of the familiar. She had been mentally escaping to the Stephen King universe for years. Now that it was time to physically escape, it seemed only logical to turn toward Castle Rock.

The trouble was, she hadn't checked the weather report. The trouble was always that Maggie didn't have a pragmatic bone in her body. She had always operated solely on her emotions, though lately, she had been working on that. So, several hours into her trek, at about two o'clock on a Saturday afternoon, Maggie found herself in the only car on I-95, with the needle hovering over the E mark, and the windshield wipers slapping frantically back and forth to little avail.

All she saw was white.

Eddie, her rat terrier-ish best friend, was curled up on the seat beside her, and she marveled at how calm he was. He certainly wasn't panicking. He was just trusting her completely to guide him through this storm.

Trying to mimic his unquestioning confidence, she prayed again, "Please, God, fix this." She had been praying that same prayer since she'd left home. She had strongly felt God telling her to leave — it wasn't much of a home anyway — so she had gotten into the car with confidence, but since then, God had been pretty quiet.

Not a peep.

Maggie looked at the gas gauge and contemplated filling up, but she didn't want Kirk to know where she was, and she didn't have any money of her own, only his plastic. It was bad enough that her Camry was titled, registered, and insured in his name.

But the snow showed no signs of letting up. She had to do something. Trying to keep one eye on the road, she opened the weather app on her phone. No signal. She scanned the radio channels, and there were precious few of them in the middle of Maine. She found no savvy weather forecaster to guide her to safety, so she switched back to her Chris Tomlin CD.

Singing along to "White Flag," making up the words she didn't yet know, she saw a green exit sign up ahead. "God, should I take that exit? Please tell me!" she pleaded, taking her foot off the gas pedal. She had pretty much decided to take the exit whether or not God piped up, but then she saw an actual white flag hanging off the exit sign and knew. There was her sign. Feeling enormous comfort, she signaled to the right and then giggled at herself for bothering to signal at all. What was she afraid of, getting rear-ended by a snowmobile?

It looked like she was driving straight into a white wall, but she was undeterred. Her tires slid a little under her, but she calmly gained control on the unnecessarily curvy exit ramp. She would be OK. She had seen a white flag.

She crawled off the interstate and smirked at a sign that read, "Welcome to Mattawooptock." Matta*what*? She searched both sides of the road for a safe place to pull over. She was tempted by the Mattawooptock Motor Inn, but that would require plastic. She drove on, wondering exactly what it was she was looking for; then she saw it.

The sign read "Open Door Church," and Maggie reasoned it couldn't get much more obvious than that. She pulled her car into a large parking lot and wondered why there were so many other cars in the lot on a snowy Saturday.

Wondering if she had stumbled onto a Christmas craft fair, she unbuckled her seatbelt and shut off her thirsty engine. Eddie looked up at her sleepily and cocked his head to one side as if to ask, "Are we home?"

Maggie rubbed his head and promised, "Be back in a flash," before she stepped out into the cold. A man was shoveling a path to the church, and Maggie panicked at the thought of human interaction. But then he smiled at her, and her heart rate slowed to a more reasonable pace.

"Nice day out!" he said.

"Sure," she said, trying to think of something more clever to say. She didn't. So she asked, "Why are there so many people here?"

He looked confused. He scanned the parking lot as if to confirm that there were in fact a lot of people there. Then he looked back at her. "Oh, I think this is about normal."

It was her turn to be confused. "Do you have a Saturday service?"

He leaned on his shovel as if it were a cane. "Not till tonight," he said, looking at her as if she was the one not making much sense.

His expression made her defensive. "Then why are all these cars here?" she asked.

"Ah!" he said as if he finally understood her question. "Those are our guests. A lot of them have cars."

He may have understood her question, but she didn't understand his answer.

"I'm Galen," he said, taking off his glove and holding out his hand toward her, "but most people call me G."

"Maggie," she said, taking his hand in her now frozen, ungloved hand. His hand felt huge as it closed around hers, and warm. "Guests?" she asked.

He shook his head. "Sorry, I'm not being a very good welcome wagon. Come on inside where it's warm, and I'll explain."

She followed him up a few snowy steps and into the warmth—a welcoming and well-lit lobby. Maggie shook the snow out of her hair. Galen pointed toward one of the few empty coat hooks on the wall and held his hand out for her coat. She gave it to him. He hung it up and then spread his arms out, "Welcome to Open Door Church. We operate a sort of homeless shelter here. Most of those cars belong to people who are staying here."

"Oh." Of all the emotions that could have popped up right then—gratitude, relief, even fear—nope, it was pride that reared its ugly head. God had led her to a homeless shelter? *Seriously, God?*

Galen looked as if he was trying to read her. "I saw your Massachusetts plates. Are you just passing through?"

She stared at him for an awkward several seconds, and then said, "No, actually. I'm pretty homeless myself."

He nodded as if he had known this, and then acting as if he was putting his left hand to the small of her back, but without actually touching her, he motioned down a hallway with his right hand, "Let me introduce you to Cari then. She'll get you set right up."

Maggie followed Galen a short distance to the doorway of a cluttered office. Behind a big desk that was absolutely buried in stacks of paper sat a petite woman with a pencil behind each ear.

"Cari! This is Maggie. She needs a place to stay. Maggie, this is Cari."

Cari looked up from her computer monitor and offered Maggie a sincere but tired smile. "Hi, Maggie. Welcome to Open Door. We're glad you're here. Have a seat," she said, pointing toward the only empty chair in the room.

"I'll get back to my shoveling, then," Galen said and gave a little wave on his way out.

"Thanks, G," Cari called after him, and reached for something in an open filing cabinet drawer.

She found what she was looking for and handed Maggie a short form to fill out. What was her name and social security number, did she have a vehicle, did she have any food allergies or dietary restrictions, was she a sex offender ...

"Sex offender?" Maggie asked, a little panicky.

"Yes," Cari said, seemingly unsurprised at the question. "We have children staying with us, so we can't allow anyone who has been convicted of a sex crime to stay here. However, if you have been convicted of one, we don't just throw you out in the cold. We help you find your way to someplace that can help you."

"Oh, no, I haven't been convicted ... of anything ... I was just ... I don't know ..."

"It's OK." Cari smiled. "Everyone asks about that question."

Maggie half-smiled back, and then filled out the form as Cari went back to stabbing at her keyboard. When Maggie finished, she handed her the form. She wasn't even sure she wanted to stay there, but she couldn't think of any other options at the moment. She vowed she would just stay for one night. She would come up with a plan tomorrow. There must be a pastor around here to help her come up with a plan, right?

"OK, great," Cari said. "We have Bible study every night at six in the sanctuary, and we ask all our guests to attend."

"OK, no prob," Maggie said, a little surprised at how excited she felt about that idea.

Chapter 2
Galen

Galen stepped back out into the cold, trying not to think about how gorgeous that woman had just been. As genuinely compassionate as he was with all the people in his church, he had reservations about having romantic feelings for a homeless person. I mean, there had to be a reason she was homeless, right?

As soon as he had the thought, he asked God to forgive him for it, and tried to focus on his shoveling. It's hard to get into trouble when thinking about shoveling. He finished shoveling the path, returned the shovel to the porch, and then headed toward his truck.

On the way to the truck though, he noticed a cute little terrier — at least, it sort of looked like a terrier — sitting behind Maggie's steering wheel. *Uh-oh*, he thought. He turned and headed back inside.

Cari and Maggie were no longer in the office, so he headed toward the women's bedrooms. He found the two women standing in the hall, and heard Maggie say, "Can I just leave him in the car? I won't bring him inside."

"No, I'm sorry," Cari said. "We can't have any pets on the premises."

Maggie looked like she was about to cry.

"Hey, Maggie," Galen interrupted, coming up behind them. "I can dogsit if you want."

Cari looked at him in surprise, but then her raised eyebrows turned into a knowing smirk as she made assumptions about his sudden love for dogs.

Maggie, though, looked skeptical.

"It's OK, really," Galen said, trying to comfort her, "she'll be in good hands."

"She's a he," Maggie corrected. "His name is Eddie."

"Eddie. Got it. Eddie will be in good hands."

Maggie deliberated, and then finally nodded.

"I'm headed home now. Do you want me to take him?" *Uh-oh*, Galen thought. The floodgates had opened. Maggie stood there weeping, which made Galen incredibly uncomfortable. He thought then that he might do just about anything to make that crying stop. "Hey," he said softly, stepping closer to her, "really, it's OK. I'm a dog guy," he said, even though he really wasn't, but he thought he might be becoming a Maggie guy. "You can trust me. I'll take him home, take him for a walk, get him something to eat, and I'll bring him back for the evening service. You can see him then." She looked up at him with giant green eyes as if she was trying to evaluate his ability to do as he was promising. He fought the urge to reach out and wipe away her tears.

"OK," she muttered. She started toward the door, and then said over her shoulder to Cari, "I'll be right back. Is that OK?"

"Of course," Cari said. "I'll be in the office."

Maggie headed outside without her coat so Galen grabbed it and handed it to her on the way to the car. "Thanks," she said. She unlocked her car and grabbed Eddie. She handed his leash and a bag of dog food to Galen. Then she buried her face in the dog's neck for what seemed like a long time, while Galen stood waiting, snow piling up on his dark hair. When Maggie kissed Eddie on the side of his snout, Galen felt something too close to jealousy. Maggie looked up, "He's my best friend. He's my only friend. He's all I have left in this world."

Galen wanted to tell her this wasn't true, but instead he said, "I understand. I will take care of him as if he were my own. He'll be OK, I promise."

Maggie sighed, kissed the dog again, and handed him to Galen. "See you tonight?"

Galen smiled. "Yes, you'll see us both tonight. Now go get warm."

She smiled back, tears still in her eyes, "Thank you." She reached into her car and grabbed a bag, and she headed toward the church.

"You bet," he said, and he watched her walk away. Then he and his new dog climbed into his truck.

On his way home, he stopped at the drugstore to get some Zyrtec. Galen was allergic to dogs.

Chapter 3

Her pride was at it again. She couldn't believe how small her room was. And it didn't smell terrific. She figured it had served as a Sunday school room in a former life. It was now home to two sets of bunk beds and a single dresser. She was allotted one drawer in the dresser and the top bunk on the left.

She knew she should be grateful, she *was* grateful, but she still felt some level of shame. She flung herself onto the top bunk, which someone had kindly made for her. *How did this happen?* she wondered. *I'm a good person. I've never hurt anyone. I even just gave my life to God. So how did I end up here in a homeless shelter in a town I can't pronounce?* On the verge of more tears, she rolled over, which brought her face to face with giant giraffe eyeballs.

The wall beside her bed portrayed a faded Noah's ark scene. She mused about how odd it is that Noah's ark is such a popular children's tale. It seemed kind of scary to her. Everyone on earth drowned. Why was that a happy story for kiddos? And sure, the animal couples were cute, but what about every single other land-roaming animal on earth? All dead! Funny how the kids' books never dwell on these angles of the story. As she tried to figure out which Bible account made for better children's art, she drifted off to sleep.

She woke to someone shaking her. She rolled over to see a young woman with bleach blond hair and brown roots. She sat up suddenly, disoriented and scared. "It's time for Bible study. You have to go," the woman said.

Maggie was annoyed at her tone, but she climbed out of bed to follow bad-hair-girl to Bible study. She was halfway down the hallway when she remembered that evening service meant a visit with Eddie. She picked up her pace.

She thought about heading straight for the parking lot, but instead opted to follow the tide into the sanctuary. The place was packed. *Just how many people live here?* she wondered. She also marveled at what a motley crew they seemed to be. People of all shapes and sizes. Some looked, well, homeless, while others looked, well, *not*. She wondered where she fell on that spectrum and realized she probably looked pretty shabby herself.

She looked around frantically for Galen, but then a bunch of musicians up front began to make a bunch of raucous, and she decided it might be more important to find a seat. Alas, she couldn't find one that had a good buffer of space on both sides; her only choice was to squeeze between a woman wearing an orange hunting hat and a dirty little kid. As she sat down, they both stood up, and Ms. Blaze Orange threw her hands up in the air as she started to sing.

Maggie stood back up and finally saw Galen—he was one of the raucous musicians up front. And they were *loud*. Two singers, a lead guitar, Galen's bass guitar, and a drum set blasted from speakers all around. Maggie didn't know the song, but she seemed to be alone on that front. Everyone in her immediate vicinity was singing, many had a hand or two up in the air, and a couple of them were dancing.

Maggie turned around to see what was happening behind her, and was a bit relieved to see that the back rows were full of people sulking and refusing to stand. *So, not everyone is this chipper around here.*

Maggie was so far out of her element. She'd never actually been to church before, and somehow, this wasn't how she had imagined it. Her friend Anna had invited her, had encouraged her to go, but Maggie always knew it would cause too much of a kerfuffle with Kirk. Instead of Maggie leaving the house, Anna had come to her, and together they had read the Bible, prayed, and talked about life. But they certainly hadn't engaged in any of this commotion.

The music seemed to go on and on. Finally, they did a Chris Tomlin song Maggie recognized. She began to sing along, and then Ms. Blaze Orange leaned over and said, "You sing like an angel." Maggie smiled in surprise. That was a new one. But then again, no one except Eddie had heard her sing in years.

Finally the music stopped, and the musicians left the stage. Galen caught her eye and smiled. She smiled back. A man in an AC/DC T-shirt got up to make some announcements. Then the pastor took the stage. She only knew he was the pastor because Mr. AC/DC called him "Pastor." Pastor was wearing a faded polo shirt and ripped blue jeans. He looked to be about 50. He was a wiry little thing who bounced around a lot while he talked. He didn't stay on stage for long, but instead came down and talked to his sheep as if they were in his living room.

The sermon was brief, but Maggie had trouble focusing because she was so overwhelmed by her surroundings. A teenager in front of her was playing Candy Crush on her phone. The guy to Candy Crush's left kept playing with his ponytail, whipping it back and forth and occasionally chewing on it. And the dirty child beside Maggie kept poking her. She thought about giving his mother a dirty look, but his mother appeared to be the mother of four other children, so Maggie figured she had other, more pressing things to worry about.

As the pastor was winding up his sermon, he asked everyone to bow their heads and close their eyes. Then he said, "If you were to die tonight, do you know where you would go? If you want to go to heaven, then repeat this prayer after me. God in heaven, thank you for sending your Son Jesus to die on the cross for my sins. I ask you to forgive my sins. I am sorry. I give my life to you now. Please take my life and use it. Amen."

Maggie peeked around to see if it was OK to look up, and apparently it was, because everyone else was doing it. She noticed the musicians had reclaimed the stage, but the pastor stayed down by the altar. As the musicians started to play softly, Pastor said, "If you prayed that prayer with me tonight, I invite you to come down front and see me. The Bible says that we should confess our faith in front of other people and you can do that tonight. You don't have to, there's no pressure, but if you'd like to, I invite you to come down front and I would like to pray with you.... Thank you brother ... anyone else?" Maggie turned around, surprised someone was coming, but someone was. And then someone else joined him. And then another. Then there were four people kneeling at the altar. Maggie's eyes welled up with tears. She had never seen anything like this.

Then the little boy poked her again. She looked down at him, ready to be annoyed, but she saw he was trying to get past her. She stepped back and let him make his way to the altar. As the tears poured down Maggie's cheeks, Ms. Blaze Orange leaned over and whispered, "Don't get too shook up, he goes down front every night."

After the service, Galen found Maggie, "Wanna go out and see Eddie?"

Maggie nodded gratefully and followed him to the door.

Outside, the snow had slowed, but the wind had picked up. She realized how "lucky" she was to have a place to sleep, a place that wasn't Kirk's.

When Eddie saw her, he smashed both front paws and a nose to the window, wagging his tail as if he was trying to put out a fire with it. Maggie was so excited to see him, she started crying again. Galen opened the door for her, and Eddie leapt into her arms. She pressed her face into his neck as he squirmed in her arms, his tail still wagging. They stood there for a minute, Maggie and Eddie content, and then Galen said, "Do you want to sit in the truck with him? It might be a smidge warmer."

"Oh yeah, sorry, thank you."

"No need to apologize," Galen said as he opened the door for her again. She hoisted herself into his truck and onto the cold leather. Galen trotted around to the other side and climbed in behind the wheel. He started the truck, which gave Maggie a momentary fright, but then she realized he was just firing up the heater.

"I can't tell you how much I appreciate this," she said, her face still pressed into Eddie's fur.

"No problem," Galen said, smiling. "Really," he added.

"So you don't mind keeping him for the night?" Maggie asked. "I hope to come up with some sort of a plan tomorrow, but right now, I'm just not sure where Eddie and I are headed next."

"Of course," Galen said, as if he understood. Then they sat there in his truck, quiet, for about 10 minutes. Maggie could have sat there longer, but she started to feel guilty about making Galen hang out in the church parking lot. Or the homeless shelter parking lot. Whichever this place was.

"Well, I guess I should let you go," Maggie said.

"You can if you want, but I'm in no hurry. Curfew is nine, and it's only 7:30, so we can sit here for another hour and a half if you'd like."

Maggie looked up sharply, "Curfew?"

"Yeah, they lock the doors at nine. So, if anyone wants to spend the night, they have to be inside by then. If they're not, they have to call Pastor. I'm not sure what happens then. They probably still let you in, but it's more of a rigmarole."

"Is that really necessary? I mean, can't people come and go as they please?"

Galen smiled, "Well, I know this is hard to believe, but sometimes we get some rough characters around here, so I think it's more of a safety thing. They want to know who is here at night, and don't want someone dangerous strolling in looking for a place to crash at midnight."

"Oh," Maggie said, a bit alarmed at his use of the word dangerous. "So, those people in church, do they all live here … I mean, are they all 'guests'?"

"Most of them," Galen nodded. "A few, like myself, live nearby."

"Oh! So this is just an ordinary church, which happens to double as a homeless shelter?"

Galen laughed, "Well, I've never heard anyone call us ordinary, but yes, we're just a church. One day our pastor ran into a man who had nowhere to go, so the pastor—his name is Dan—just let him sleep at the church. And that's when it started."

"So, what's that building?" Maggie said, pointing across the parking lot at a small ranch house dwarfed by the oddly-shaped church.

"That's the parsonage, where Pastor lives."

"Ah," she said. "Does he live alone?"

"Yeah, his wife died a few years ago. Cancer. Shortly before the church started accepting overnighters."

"Oh, wow," she said. "How sad. That poor man."

"Yep. He's an incredible man of faith though. Really walks the talk, you know?"

"Yeah … well, I should let you get home."

"OK," he said, handing her a slip of paper. "Here's my cell. Call anytime if you need anything, even if you just want to check on your little pal here."

She sighed and smiled at him, suddenly noticing how gentle he looked. He sort of looked like a six-foot tall teddy bear. His broad shoulders made him look even bigger than he was. "Again, I don't know how to thank you."

"No worries, really, I've done far more obnoxious favors for far less pleasant people," he said, and then she thought she saw a hint of a blush, but it was hard to see anything, their only light traveling from tired parking lot bulbs through falling snow.

"OK," Maggie said. She gave Eddie one more kiss, then set him on the seat beside her and looked at Galen. "Good night then?"

"Good night," Galen answered. "Talk to you tomorrow."

She stepped back out into the cold and walked to the church. When she reached the door, she turned to wave. They were still sitting there, truck idling, but as she opened the door, her only two friends in the world drove away.

Chapter 4

"So what's your story?"

Maggie was lying in her bunk, after lights out, when a voice below her startled her out of her thoughts. The voice belonged to Jackie, an older woman with long, gray, stringy hair and several missing teeth. She had introduced herself earlier, and had seemed nice enough. "Maggie?"

"Yeah?" Maggie said, because she didn't know what else to say.

"What's your story?"

"I don't really have one." Maggie wasn't trying to be enigmatic; she just really didn't find her story all that exciting.

"Everybody has a story, sugar," her bunkmate said, and in the soft light, she saw Bleach Blonde across the room prop herself up on her elbow to watch the exchange.

Maggie considered making up a story, but decided she wasn't creative enough. "I don't know … I just … I don't have a job right now and don't have any place to stay." She left out the part about *never* having a job, despite being 25.

"So you drove all the way from Massachusetts?" her bunkmate said, almost critically, as Maggie silently cursed her license plates. "Don't they have homeless shelters in Mass?" Maggie heard Bleach Blonde snort, and was annoyed.

"I just needed to get away for a while, so I asked God where to go, and he brought me here."

Crickets.

Apparently, Maggie had figured out how to bring an abrupt end to an interrogation. Just claim divine intervention. Maggie rolled over to face the giraffe. It was too dark to see him, but knowing he was there brought her an odd comfort.

She was almost asleep when she heard Bleach Blonde softly say, probably to herself, "That's kind of how I got here too."

The next morning, Maggie woke to the smell of bacon and coffee. She reasoned she must be close to the kitchen, but then she saw Bleach Blonde had actually brought some bacon, wrapped in a napkin, and some coffee into the room.

Maggie swung her legs off the bed and said, more crankily then she meant to, "Bacon at a homeless shelter? I was expecting beans and rice."

Bleach Blonde looked up at her. "Yeah, it's Sunday, and they always make a big breakfast for Sunday morning. Some of the church folk come to eat with us. Here, I brought you coffee."

"Thanks," Maggie said. She wasn't really a coffee drinker, but it seemed like a good time to start. "So, you just squirrel away some extra bacon for the rest of the week?"

Bleach Blonde looked hurt. "No," she said, staring at the bacon, "I brought it for your dog."

Maggie felt like a pile of poop. "Oh, sorry ... well, thank you. And Eddie thanks you. He'll be thrilled." Maggie jumped off the bed. "What's your name again?" she asked, not sure if she'd actually heard it yet.

"Harmony."

"Wow, that's a pretty name. I'm kind of jealous."

"Don't be," Harmony said, "my name kind of calls attention to the fact that there's not much harmony in my life."

"Ah, good point ... so, is there a bathroom nearby?"

"Yeah, follow me."

"Hang on, just a sec." Maggie realized she was about to leave her bedroom and see God knows how many people on the way to the bathroom, so she hurriedly put on a bra, marveling at how strange it was to bra up before a shower. "OK," she said, and followed Harmony out the door and down the hall to a women's restroom, with a handwritten sign on the door that read "NO MEN ALLOWED IN WOMEN'S BATHROOM."

The restroom was tiny, with only two stalls and one sink.

When she got back to her room, she asked Harmony, "Are there any showers?"

"Yep!" Harmony declared. Maggie sensed that Harmony enjoyed feeling needed. Harmony guided her through a few twists and turns to a closed door with two women waiting beside it. They looked grouchy, and kind of scary.

"Oh, there's a line?" Maggie said, mostly to herself.

"Yeah, always. But this isn't bad," Harmony explained. "Earlier it was much longer. Church starts in half an hour, so most of those who want to have already showered."

"Oh, OK," Maggie said, "thanks," and she leaned against the wall, resigning herself to wait her turn, like a good homeless person.

Ten minutes later, one woman, her hair wrapped in a towel, stepped out of the bathroom and said, "There's no hot water." This reminded Maggie that she hadn't brought a towel. She also realized that she was out of time if she was going to make it to the church service. She wanted to get there early, to see Eddie and give him his bacon treat. Hardly able to believe it, she realized she was about to go to church without a shower. This horrified her, but she was more than a little comforted by the idea of how much more this would horrify Kirk.

She returned to her room and fished out a makeup compact. She flipped it open to survey the damage. It was significant. She tried to smooth her hair into a ponytail, thenrealized that didn't help much, and opted for a bun instead. Yesterday's eye makeup and ample tears had joined forces to make her look like a homicidal raccoon. She rooted around in her bag to find some eye makeup remover, but then realized she had no cotton balls. She decided to head back to the tiny bathroom, where there was a real mirror and some toilet paper.

On her way there, she ran into Galen.

"Hey!" Galen said, smiling.

"Hey," Maggie said, wishing he hadn't found her just yet.

"I was just looking for you. Did you want to see Eddie before the service?"

"Definitely … can I meet you by the door in just a sec?"

"Oh, of course," and he turned and walked away. She scooted into the bathroom for some quick primitive primping. Then she scurried back to her room, grabbed her bacon, and tried to navigate her way back to the front door. *Man, there sure are a lot of hallways for a church,* she thought and then she found Galen waiting patiently by the door.

"Thanks," she said, "sorry about that."

"No worries," Galen said as they stepped out into the cold. They silently walked to Galen's truck, and he opened the truck door for her. Eddie, looked up, surprised to see her, and then completely forgot about her when he caught wind of the treat in her hand. She scooped him up in her arms and hand-fed him, kissing him repeatedly on the top of his head as he tried to swallow the bacon without chewing.

"I fed him, I swear," Galen said.

Maggie laughed, "Yeah, he's kind of a little pig." Then she looked at Galen, trying to think of something to say, "So do you come to all the services?"

Galen laughed as if that was absurd. "No, I'm a Saturday night guy. I just came this morning to see you." Galen quickly looked at the ground, kicked at something she couldn't see and said, "I mean, so that Eddie could see you."

"Oh, well, we sure do appreciate it, don't we, Eddie?" she asked, pushing her face into his neck again.

"But we should get inside, service is about to start, and I don't want you to get into trouble."

Maggie looked up, "Seriously? I would get into trouble?"

"Well, nothing serious, but the only real rule about living here is that you go to church every day."

"Oh," she paused, "I see." She opened the door, placed Eddie back into the truck, and kissed him once more on the head. She shut the door and turned back to Galen. "Then I guess I should go to church. Are you staying?"

"Might as well," Galen said, looking a little uncomfortable. They turned and walked back to the church, just as the music started up.

The sanctuary was packed. They squeezed into the back, among the less enthusiastic worshippers. Maggie noticed a pungent odor, but couldn't identify its source. She also noticed there were new musicians on the stage. She had to practically holler into Galen's ear, "They have a whole new band for Sunday mornings?"

He nodded, and then said into her ear, "We call them worship teams, and yes, we have several. We rotate, take turns." His breath felt hot on her ear, and sent little shivers up her spine. She stepped back, alarmed at the shivers, and looked at him. Apparently unaware of her shivers, he smiled and looked toward the front. He started to sing, but she couldn't hear his voice. The band, er, *worship team*, was that loud.

After several songs, they sat down, and she noticed several of the men were staring at her. More like leering. Some of them looked downright frightful, and without thinking about it, she scooted closer to Galen and tried to keep her eyes front.

Chapter 5
Galen

Why is she sitting so close to me?

Galen tried to focus on what Pastor Dan was saying, but he wasn't having much success. This girl had him beyond distracted. *She is practically cuddled right up to me. Is she trying to send a message? Could she actually like me? No, she's just manipulating the only guy she knows with a job. Wait, how does she know I have a job? She just knows I have a truck and a place to sleep at night. Am I being a jerk or am I being discerning? Why do I have to overanalyze everything?*

"Achoo!" It came out of nowhere, exploding loudly enough to embarrass him.

"God bless you," she whispered.

He knew another one was coming, and he tried to stifle it, but he didn't have much luck. "Achoo!" he shouted into the crook of his arm.

"God bless you again," she whispered. "You're not allergic to Eddie, are you?"

Galen silent-chuckled. *Of course not! How absurd!*

Oh no, there was still another one coming. Was he actually going to have to leave the service? "Achoo!"

She looked at him, appearing genuinely concerned. He tried to smile, but was too scared of bringing on another attack. It had been a rough night. He'd spread a blanket on the floor for Eddie, but Eddie continued to try to jump on the bed. Each time, Galen gently placed him on the floor, but as soon as Galen lay back down, Eddie would jump on the bed again.

Galen lived in a studio apartment over his garage, so the only room with a door was the bathroom. He'd gotten up, made a little nest out of bath towels, and locked Eddie in the bathroom. But then Eddie had begun to whine. Actually it was more like a wail. Galen couldn't believe how much noise such a small dog could make. After a few minutes of Eddie frantically scratching at the bathroom door and wailing at the top of his little lungs, Galen got up to spring him from his cell. As soon as he cracked the door open, Eddie shot out past Galen's legs and leapt onto the bed like a four-legged Olympic gymnast. Then he spun around three times before curling up into a ball and collapsing on Galen's pillow.

Galen sighed and surrendered. He wearily climbed back into bed, rolled over so the back of his head was pressed up against the dog's butt, and thanked God Maggie didn't own a Great Dane. He never would have been able to fall asleep like that, but he was positively stoned on Benadryl.

Only a few hours later, he woke to Eddie, whining again and stepping on his head. He pushed Eddie off, and the little bugger ran to the apartment door and began to scratch at it. Galen assumed this meant it was potty time, so he staggered around in the dark, trying to locate the tiny leash and his boots. He finally got them both dressed and Eddie pulled him out the door, down the stairs into his garage, and out the garage door into the cold. Then Galen stood in the cold while Eddie spent at least ten minutes doing figure eights and sniffing snow. Finally, Eddie found a worthy spot and did his business. Then he dragged Galen back toward the door, hurriedly, as if this little excursion had all been Galen's idea.

Back in bed at last, Galen couldn't fall back asleep, despite the Benadryl. He prayed, "Lord, if I stand any chance with this woman, please make it happen. And if I don't stand a chance, please take these feelings away from me."

Now, trying to listen to Pastor Dan's sermon, Galen remembered that prayer, and silently repeated it.

Chapter 6

Maggie thoroughly enjoyed Pastor Dan's sermon on The Prodigal Son. The service concluded with a salvation message similar to the one she had heard the night before. The dirty kid went down front again.

After the altar call, Mr. AC/DC, who was now wearing a Kiss T-shirt, got up and invited everyone to stay for lunch.

Maggie looked at Galen, "Do you usually stay for lunch?"

"I'm not usually here on Sundays, but sure, I could eat," he said, playfully patting his stomach, which only slightly protruded over his jeans.

"Well, I'm starving. Want to join me?" She hoped she wasn't being too flirty. She didn't mean to give her new friend any ideas. She was just terrified of going to lunch alone.

"Of course," Galen said, and stepped back so she could step out into the aisle.

When she did so, she noticed several of the aforementioned men still ogling her. She leaned back toward Galen and whispered, "Why is everyone staring at me?"

"Because you're a beautiful woman, and some of these guys don't have great social skills." She was glad her back was toward him, because his comment caught her off-guard.

She couldn't remember anyone ever calling her beautiful before. Certainly not Kirk. And she certainly didn't consider herself beautiful. Plain Jane was more like it. Wavy, unruly brown hair. Her nose was too small and her mouth was too big. She did think her green eyes were kind of special, but no one had ever confirmed that.

She followed the tide out of the sanctuary and down some stairs, into a rather creepy looking basement that smelled delicious. They lined up cafeteria style, and some clean-looking people wearing hairnets served her some food. She was impressed by how efficient it all was.

"Do these people work here?" she asked Galen.

"No," he said. "Well, sort of. They work, but no one pays them. Most people who are here for a while find a way to volunteer, to chip in somehow."

"Oh," she said, panicking a little. Another reason she had to get out of there. She didn't really have any useful skills to chip in with.

They found a seat, which wasn't easy. Maggie ended up squished against a wall, her head almost touching a shelf overhanging the table. Galen was beside her, and two disgruntled-looking older gentlemen, who looked suspiciously alike, sat across from them.

"So," one of them said to Galen, "who's the little lady?"

"This is Maggie. Maggie, this is Hershel and Dale."

"Hi," Maggie said.

Hershel, or Dale, she wasn't sure who was who, said, "How's the wrench business?"

Maggie thought he said "wench business" and was appalled. *Did he just call me a wench?*

But Galen only nodded and said, "Good, good."

What on earth?

One of the men took a mouthful of mashed potatoes and then spit some of it back out as he said, "I can be quite handy with a wrench myself."

Oh! Wrench!

Galen nodded again, "Good, cause I could use some help with the church bus. Apparently the rear brakes are making a wicked racket."

"Oh, yeah, well," Hershel/Dale stammered, "well, I've got an appointment today."

Galen smiled craftily. "Oh, no worries. I wasn't planning on it today. I can wait till you're available."

At that, Hershel/Dale fell silent and focused on their plates. The extended quiet made Maggie uncomfortable, so after a while, she asked, "Are you two brothers?"

They laughed as if that was the funniest thing they'd ever heard, spraying mashed potatoes and corn too close to Maggie's plate. "Nah, I don't think so, though, knowing Dale's mother, it's possible!" She didn't really get the joke, but she was glad to learn which one was Dale.

Dale elbowed Hershel in the ribs. "Don't you talk about my mother! Unless you're a paying customer!" At this, they both laughed again. The air was positively loaded with flying food particles. Maggie pushed her plate away, and waited for Galen to finish.

He seemed to take her cue though, and asked, "Done already?"

"Yes," she said, and before she had even pronounced the "s," Dale had snagged her bread from her plate.

She must have given him a dirty look because he said, "Sorry, this bread is just like Hershel's mother used to make," and they were at it again, laughing and spraying. She was glad she wasn't in charge of cleaning the dining area. Galen showed Maggie where to return their plates and silverware, and then they headed upstairs.

"Where does all the food come from?" Maggie asked.

"Grocery stores," Galen replied.

"How can they afford it?" Maggie asked. "Someone must be putting more in the offering plate than I am."

"Oh no," Galen said, "the grocery stores just give us stuff. Lots of it. Stuff that's almost expired, stuff that's not selling. I don't think we've ever gone a day without enough food."

"Wow," Maggie said, impressed.

He stopped at the top of the stairs, looking nervous all of a sudden. "So, um, I figured you wanted to hang out with Eddie for a while. And there's a game on this afternoon I kinda wanted to watch. Do you, um, wanna come over and watch it with me?"

This sounded entirely reasonable, but before she could even say yes, he added, "It's not a date or anything, I mean, you're totally safe with me." He looked positively sweet as he was saying this, and it occurred to her that he was a genuinely nice man. She wasn't sure she had really known one of those before.

"I would love to," she said. "But would you mind if I took a shower first?"

"Of course not," Galen said, sounding relieved. "I'll go back down and chat with Hershel and Dale."

Maggie laughed. "OK then, you're a brave man. I'll be down in a few."

Chapter 7
Galen

As Galen headed down the stairs to the church basement, he heard a tremendous crash. He assumed Charlie had dropped a tub of dishes again. Then he heard Rita scream a long string of expletives, presumably at poor Charlie. Galen shook his head. *It's only by the grace of God that no one gets knifed in this kitchen,* he thought.

Dale and Hershel were right where he'd left them, still sitting side by side like the world's weirdest twins. He plopped down across from them. Dale gave him a huge, creepy grin, "So, tell us the truth, G, you doing the tango with that little honey?"

Galen rolled his eyes. "Enough," he said, and he gave them a look that said he meant it.

Dale didn't take the hint. "So, where's she from? What's her deal? Why's she here?"

Galen ignored him.

Hershel didn't. "Well, Dale, I'm assuming she's here 'cause she needed a roof over her head."

That ended the Maggie portion of the conversation, and the two began to fervently complain about the price of cigarettes. Galen sat there, waiting, his knee bouncing up and down. Every five seconds, he glanced at the stairs, but they remained full of people who were not Maggie. He started to panic. *Maybe she forgot? Maybe she changed her mind? And why am I so nervous?*

Finally, Maggie appeared on the stairs, looking more beautiful than ever. Her hair fell beyond her shoulders in wet waves that shone in the fluorescent lights. She wore jeans and a baggie blouse, no jewelry or makeup in sight, and it occurred to him for the first time that maybe he preferred the low-maintenance type.

He tried to sound casual. "You ready?"

She nodded. Dale said something goofy, and both men laughed, but Galen ignored them both as he made his way to the stairs. He tried to think of something to say on their way to the truck, and failed. But that seemed to be OK as she soon became totally occupied with Eddie.

"So, how was your night?" Galen tried.

"Actually, much better than I thought it would be. I slept like a log. How about you?"

"Yep, a log sounds about right," he lied.

"Can I ask you a question?" she asked.

Oh no, what has she heard? "Shoot."

"Why do they call you G?"

He sighed with relief. "Well, over the years, my name has gotten me a lot of grief. So I used to ask people to just call me G. But now I don't really care. You can call me Galen," he finished, wishing she would. He liked the way his name sounded in her voice.

"Ah, that makes sense," Maggie said, "but please don't call me Margaret."

It wasn't that funny, but he laughed as if it was.

"So what kind of a name is Galen? I mean, I like it, but I've never heard it before."

"My mother's parents were Gale and Waylon. So I'm Galen."

"Oh, cool."

"I guess.... So, you like football?"

"Not really."

"Ah, good to know you're not perfect," he said, and instantly regretted it. Her face sort of froze in a half-smile, and he knew he'd pushed too hard. *Don't be crazy. This girl is like 10 years younger than you and is practically a supermodel. You're just the dogsitter, Galen.*

She interrupted his self-scolding with, "Thanks again, Galen. I can't tell you how grateful I am for your friendship."

Friendship. So there it is. OK, well, at least he knew. He would end his ridiculous attempts at flirting and just accept this for what it was, a friendship. She just needed his help. He would help her, and try to enjoy it.

"You bet," he managed.

A few silent minutes later, he pulled into his driveway.

"G's Automotives," she said, reading the sign on his garage. "You live here?"

"Yep, there's an apartment upstairs." He pressed a button on his visor to open the garage door and parked inside. He handed her the end of Eddie's leash and said, "You want to take him out for a minute? He's been in the truck a while."

She nodded and grabbed her little friend.

Galen practically ran inside to turn the heat up and make sure there wasn't anything embarrassing lying around. He couldn't find anything, but that didn't mean it wasn't there. He was in the middle of another sneezing fit when he heard her downstairs. "Up here!" he yelled.

She entered his apartment and her eyes scanned the place, which made him nervous. He took her coat, and asked, "You want anything to eat or drink? I noticed you didn't exactly binge at lunch, despite claiming starvation."

"Yeah, I'll admit, Hershel and Dale kind of spooked me."

He laughed. "Yeah, they spook me a little too, but they kind of grow on you. Besides, Dale is a Vietnam vet, so I cut him some slack. And Hershel is a recovering heroin addict. So, food and drink?"

"Nah, I'm OK, thanks."

"OK, well, let me know if you change your mind. Make yourself comfortable," he said, pointing to the couch. She looked around as if looking for somewhere else to sit. "Sorry, not much furniture. I don't get much company up here," he explained, as he sat on the far end of the sofa. Any closer to the edge and he would actually be sitting on the armrest.

"No worries," she said, sitting down at the other end. She'd barely settled before Eddie tried to climb onto her lap. She pushed him off. The pup looked as if she'd smacked him.

Galen said, "It's fine, let him up. He's already slept on my pillow."

"Seriously? I guess I'm not as special as I thought. So, who's playing?" and she turned her attention to the television.

Galen fought back the urge to tell her exactly how special she seemed to be, but answered her football question instead.

"Aha," she said, and he guessed she had never heard of either team.

They fell into a tolerable silence, both watching the game. At least, they were both staring at it. He wasn't sure if she was watching.

"You warm enough?" he asked.

"Yeah, thanks," she said, without looking at him.

Could this be any more awkward?

Several interminable minutes later, it was halftime. He figured halftime would be at least half again as uncomfortable as the first half had been, but she spoke right up to fill the silence, "So, I was supposed to figure out my life today. Want to help?"

While Galen was genuinely excited she had asked, he was also quite certain he wasn't up to the task of figuring out her life. He reminded himself to just stick to biblical advice. When in doubt, quote Paul. "Sure, what's up?"

"Well," she took a deep breath, as if she was about to talk a lot, "I don't really want to live in a homeless shelter. Or a church. Or a church slash homeless shelter. I need to figure out a way to, you know, live on my own. I've never done that before."

"Huh," he said, and then stared at her as he tried to think of something applicable the Apostle had once said, ever. He considered "I can do all things through Christ" but then didn't know which translation she preferred, and if it was the new NIV, that could be problematic. He shook his head, as if that would make him smarter. "Well, I think I need a little more info. You're from Massachusetts right? Did you have a job there?"

"No," she answered quickly. "I've never had a job. And I don't want to live in Mass anymore. Anywhere else would be fine. I just need a job, a way to support myself."

"What about your folks? Where do they live?"

Maggie sighed as if she was tired of telling the story. "I never knew my father. My mom died when I was ten. I was raised by my grandmother, but she died a few years ago too. I'm alone."

"OK," Galen said, feeling like a big jerk. "Well, do you have any employable skills?"

"Not really," she said, looking at the ceiling as if answers were written on it. "I mean, I'm pretty smart. Book smart anyway, not much common sense, or so I've been told. I went to beauty school, but I wasn't very good at it. Never did anything with it. And it's been years. If I actually cut someone's hair now, I'm pretty sure they'd sue me." She laughed, and it was beautiful. He noticed he liked her teeth, and then he felt weird about that. "Or at least, they would never come back."

"OK, well, what are you willing to do? Maybe you could get a job working in a salon, not as a barber, or whatever they're called, but cleaning or something? Or for that matter, cleaning anywhere? Maybe even washing dishes, or waitressing?"

Her eyes lit up a little. "Yes! I am actually an excellent cleaner. Good point! And I wouldn't mind waitressing, except that I'm kind of scared of people, and when they are mean to me, I cry."

"Oh," Galen said, not sure whether she was exaggerating, and hoping that she was. While he didn't plan on ever being mean to her, this gave him extra motivation to be careful. "Well, you have a car right? That's a big help. So you don't have to find a job within walking distance."

Her face fell, and he feared tears were imminent. "I don't really have a car. I mean, it's mine, but I didn't buy it. And it's not registered in my name. So, when Kirk—he's my ex—when he figures out I'm really gone, he's going to want the car back."

Galen sat staring at her, feeling as if he had just stepped into dangerous waters. "Your ex? As in ex-husband?"

"Oh no," she said quickly. "We never got married, though we were together forever it seems. We lived together though," she said, looking down at her hands as if ashamed of something.

"Maggie," Galen said, surprised at the softness in his own voice. "I'm the last person who will ever judge you. Ever."

She didn't raise her head, just her eyes, and looked at him. It was unnerving.

"Well," he continued, "I don't know Kirk, but … well, I don't mean to pry, but did you take anything else? Money? Stuff? Is Eddie his?"

"No, why?"

"I'm just thinking that maybe if you called and asked, you know, if he knew you weren't trying to rip him off—not that you would do that—I'm just saying, if you called, maybe he would let you put the car in your name. Is it paid for? Is he still making payments?" Galen took a deep breath, suddenly exhausted from all the talking. He realized that was the most he'd talked in months. And then, there they were. The tears. Despite himself, he groaned out loud. "I'm sorry, I didn't mean to upset you."

"No, no, you didn't," she smiled through her tears. "Of course it's not your fault. I'm just mad. I'm mad that I can't have my car. I'm mad at myself for taking the car. I'm mad at Kirk. I'm mad at myself for staying with Kirk."

Wow. He was so glad he wasn't a woman. That was a lot of madness. "OK, well, if you don't want to call, how about I just return the car for you? I won't even tell him where I found it."

Maggie looked at him like he was brilliant. "Because you have a tow truck."

Galen wasn't sure whether that was a question or statement, but he said, "Yes."

"But I don't have any money to pay you."

"No prob. Just give me the address, and I can leave tomorrow."

Chapter 8
Galen

He got to church early Monday morning, and hooked onto her car. True to her word, she had cleaned it out and left the keys. Then he headed inside to find her. Hanging up his coat, he realized this might be difficult. He'd never actually wandered into the church at a random hour to find a female. Where would she be? What if she was still in bed in a room with three other sleeping women? So he did what everybody does at Open Door when there is a crisis. He went to find Cari. Of course, she was in her office. Of course, she looked busy.

"Good morning, Cari."

She looked up, "Oh, good morning, G," she said, looking even more stressed out than usual.

"Everything OK?"

She grunted, which sounded hilarious coming from such a petite woman. "I just received a tip that the code guy is on his way. I'm trying to figure out how many guests were here last time he popped by, because he said then there were too many. But I can't figure out how many were here," she shuffled through some more papers. "I really need to keep better records, but it's impossible, people coming and going so fast, and people leave without telling me."

Galen didn't really follow what she was saying, so he just walked over and calmly put his hand on the pile of papers, as if to force her to take a break. She looked up. "Anything I can do to help?"

"Yes," she said.

Galen stood waiting for more information. It didn't come. "OK, what?"

"I don't know," she said, and she looked as though she was going to cry.

Oh no, more tears. "OK, what's the worst thing that could happen? He's not going to kick all these people out into the cold, is he? Won't he just give us another warning, and then file some more paperwork, and then disappear again for a while?"

"I honestly don't know, G, he really seems to have it in for us. He's already threatened to involve law enforcement. And where would all these people go?"

Her voice cracked then, and Galen steeled himself against the tears he knew he couldn't stop. "So when is he getting here?" Galen asked.

"Not sure," Cari replied. "Sometime this morning."

"Well, how do you know at all?"

Cari looked sheepish. "Um … I got a tip."

"Yeah, you said that. But from who?"

"I sort of have a spy in his office."

"You got a tip from your spy? What are we, the CIA?" Galen gave a little half-laugh.

She didn't see the humor apparently. "No, we are not CIA. There's just a Christian in his office who wants to help us. But I guess we're breaking all sorts of codes here. Which really, we're not, because there are no building codes for churches, except that we need fire exits and wheelchair ramps, which we have … sort of …" Galen nodded, knowing she was referencing that their ramps were absolute death traps. The kids dared one another to run up and down them. "But homeless shelters do have codes."

"Do you know what they are?"

"Why, are you going to wire in some smoke detectors before he gets here?"

Galen frowned.

"Sorry, I'm a bit snippy today. Still trying to quit smoking." She lifted her sleeve to show him her nicotine patch.

He nodded. "So, do any of us know what these codes are?"

"I can't remember it all, but we need to have a bed per person. No one can sleep on the floor. We need to have one toilet per ten people. Hard-wired smoke detectors. Sprinklers. Back-up generator for heat … But if a homeless shelter has fewer than 20 people, then none of these rules apply. At least I think he said 20. I don't know, it's like calculus."

"So what if we load everybody up on the bus and take them to the mall for a few hours?"

Cari laughed. Her laugh was adorable. Like a high-pitched little cackle. "Are you serious?"

"I don't know? Would it work? He shows up, there's only 18 people here. We'll call it a field trip."

She frowned. "Is it dishonest?"

Galen sighed, "I don't know. Probably. But don't lie. Just keep insisting that we're a church. Tell him you don't know how many people are here. *Do you* actually know how many people are here? I mean, honestly? I sure don't."

"OK, we can decide whether it's ethical later. For now, just go round everybody up and get them out of here. It'll be a field trip. Just coincidental. Christmas is coming …" She began to talk faster, and turned to unlock the safe behind her. She withdrew two handfuls of cash and practically threw the money at Galen. It looked like a lot, but he knew it was mostly ones and fives. One doesn't get a lot of big bills in the offering plate when one's congregation is predominantly homeless. "Split this up between them and tell them to do their Christmas shopping." She stopped and looked at him. "Well? What are you waiting for? Go get a couple of the guys together and round everybody up. Don't tell them why."

"Where's Pastor?" Galen asked, suddenly worried he was the mastermind behind a terribly evil plot.

"I have no idea. He doesn't need to know. Let's go, G, chop chop!"

Despite his ethical dilemma, Galen smiled at her sudden shrill bossiness. He turned to go, and as he walked out the door, she called, "Be sure to leave some behind, so it looks realistic!"

Galen had only taken five steps when he ran into Dale and Hershel. Marveling again that these two were *always* together, he said, "Hey, guys, wanna go to the mall and do some Christmas shopping?"

Dale looked at him as though he had lost his mind. "What am I gonna pay with, my only four teeth I got left?"

Hershel laughed, "No thanks, man."

"No, really, I've got some cash. Let's round some people up and go to the mall. Monday morning field trip!" Galen said, trying to make it sound fun.

Hershel and Dale looked at each other, appearing to telepathically communicate for a bit before simultaneously shrugging their shoulders and then looking back at Galen. "Sure. Why not?" Hershel said, "Might be fun to descend on the mall. We can all go into Bath & Body Works at the same time and use up all the testers."

"OK great," Galen said, "go find some others. I'll meet you at the bus. Tell them I've got money."

Hershel and Dale turned to go and Galen heard Dale ask Hershel, "Am I too big for the carousel?"

Galen stopped at the office again to get the bus key from Cari. "Is it working?" she asked.

"Yep, I got Dale and Hershel on it," Galen answered.

"Perfect!" she declared, handing Galen the keys.

Galen got the bus started, and then headed back inside. He was hardly in the door when he encountered a short, squat woman he didn't remember seeing before. She looked young for the walker she was leaning on. "I hear there's a trip to the mall?" she asked him.

"Yeah," he said, "wait right here, we'll leave in just a minute on the bus."

He walked by her to find more recruits, and she called after him, "Great! I need new skivvies!"

He shuddered and continued down the hall. As he rounded a corner that really needed some mirrors, he smashed into Hershel. "All the men are on their way up, G."

"Good," Galen said. "What about the women and children?"

"Are you nuts?" Hershel said. "I'm not going into the hens' wing this early in the morning."

Galen sighed, "Come on. I don't really want to do it either, but let's go together. We'll be safer that way."

"Can't," Hershel said. "Dale's waitin' for me."

Galen rolled his eyes. "He can wait like two more seconds," he said, grabbing Hershel's arm and dragging him down the hall.

They knocked on the first door they came to. "Good morning, ladies," Galen said through the door. "It's G and Hershel. Could we speak to one of you for a moment?"

A woman named Jenny opened the door. "What's up?" she asked. Jenny was on Galen's worship team, so her familiar face relieved much of his anxiety.

"Cari gave me a little bit of cash. We're taking a field trip to the mall. Could you run around to the girls' rooms and see if anyone wants to join us?"

"Sure," Jenny said. "When are we leaving?"

"As fast as you can round 'em up."

"OK, sure. Meet you at the bus?"

"Yep. Thanks, Jenny."

Galen and Hershel headed outside. When they got to the bus, Galen panicked. He wasn't sure what the bus's maximum capacity was, but he was pretty sure they were exceeding it. And he didn't see hardly any women. He wondered just how many people had slept at the church last night, and what was he going to do if he couldn't get everyone on the bus?

He walked back inside to consult with Cari and met a surge of women and children coming out the door. He began to panic that the great homeless shelter escape caper was going to fail. He got to the office and asked, "Will everybody fit in the bus?"

Cari looked up. "Probably?"

"Or probably not," Galen said. "It's completely packed with people, and there are still people waiting to get on."

"Shoot," Cari said. She put her head in her hands.

Suddenly, another alarm went off in Galen's mind. "Who is going to drive the bus?"

"What?" Cari said alarmed. "You can't drive it?"

"Well, I probably could, but I don't have a bus license."

"OK, I guess I've got to call Pastor after all. You go get some volunteers to wait for the next run. Tell them we're going in two rounds, that we can't all go at once. This building sounds absolutely silent. I don't think there's anyone left."

"Really?" Galen said with not a little snark. "You tell a bunch of homeless people you're going to give them money, and some of them choose to stay behind?"

Cari didn't seem to notice his tone. "Figure it out, G. Go out to the bus and get some of them back inside. This was all your idea. I'll call Pastor."

This was all his idea. He vowed to never have another idea, ever. He really hadn't planned to spend all day shuttling homeless people back and forth to the mall. He did have a business to run. And a car to deliver to Massachusetts. He sighed. As he approached the bus, he saw Maggie among those waiting to get on.

"What on earth is going on?" she asked him.

"I'll explain later, but right now I need your help." He climbed onto the bus, where everyone was apparently engaged in a shouting competition. One by one, they saw him, and looked up. Quieting down, they stared at him expectantly.

"So," he began, not really sure what he was going to say next, "we've got a bit of a problem. We don't all fit. So we're going to make two trips. I need some volunteers to wait with Maggie," he said pointing outside at Maggie, "for the second round." He looked at Maggie and she didn't look perturbed, much to his relief. He returned his gaze to the full bus and marveled at how the mothers were managing to balance multiple children on their laps. "So, any takers?"

No one spoke.

"If no one volunteers, I'm going to have to pick people. Somebody needs to wait for the next round, and we need to hurry or we won't have time for two trips." He paused and waited. Nothing. "Come on, guys, the last shall be first, right?" At that, a few people stood up, including the mom with five children, so that sped up the head count. They filed off the bus, and Galen smiled at the little boy who got saved every night. "Thank you," he said, and the little boy nodded. "OK," Galen said, "that's 11. We need about six more. Come on people."

Nothing. As he waited, Pastor stepped onto the bus behind him, looking tired and disheveled. He gave Galen a moderately dirty look and slid into the driver's seat. Then he hollered, looking up into the mirror, "Hershel, Dale, Jenny, Barbara, Steve, and José, off the bus. You're in the next round."

"No fair ..." Dale began, but then he saw Hershel getting up without complaint, and so he followed suit.

The second round walked back to the church and the bus pulled out of the parking lot. Everybody resumed their shouting contest, and Galen stared morosely out the window. He made eye contact with Maggie and couldn't muster a smile. He just nodded. She nodded back, and went inside.

Chapter 9
Mr. Lance Pouliot,
Code Enforcement Officer

He pulled into the church parking lot and smiled when he saw all the cars. *Aha!* he thought, *I will surely nail them this time. No way that many people sleep at a church. This is a homeless shelter, plain and simple.* He noticed the car with Massachusetts plates hooked up to the tow truck and smirked. No surprise. Another free rider getting their car repo'd.

He walked into the church and found the office lady in her usual spot. "Good morning," he said.

"Good morning," she said, without making eye contact.

"I'm here to do an inspection—"

She interrupted him, "I'm not sure why you think you need to inspect a church?"

He grimaced. "We both know this is more than a church. You have homeless people sleeping here, and from the looks of the parking lot, quite a few of them."

"We have guests here, sir, and we get no funding from the government. We are a church. We are a group of people who work together to worship and serve God. Surely you can see the good in that?"

"I'm not here for a political debate, but I will say that when you give lazy people handouts, you perpetuate laziness. *Surely, you can see the truth in that?"* He knew he was practically snarling, but he couldn't help it. How could this woman be so naïve? "I'll just have a look around and be out of your way." He turned to go and was immensely annoyed when he realized she was following him.

He headed toward the sanctuary. He had heard that people actually slept on the pews in here, but he saw no evidence of that. He looked around for pillows or blankets, but saw nothing. It looked like an ordinary, albeit well-used, sanctuary. Frustrated, he turned toward the rest of the building.

When this church had first lost its mind and started accepting overnight "guests," they had added a misshapen, ramshackle "wing" to their church. They hadn't hired contractors or anything. There were just a bunch of strange people out there hammering away, and the layout of the wing proved their ignorance. He weaved around, looking for signs of life, but saw only empty bunk beds.

He turned to his shadow, "Where is everybody?"

"Oh, around," Cari said evasively. "Our guests don't spend all day in bed, Mr. Pouliot. Nor do we keep track of their whereabouts. They are guests, not prisoners."

"Uh-huh," he said, and moved on. Still no one. He exited the addition and headed back into the old church building. He heard some voices and headed down another dimly lit hallway. He found a family in one of the rooms. The kids were sitting on the floor playing with blocks. A woman lay in bed reading. He was surprised she could read. When she saw him, she sat up.

She looked him up and down, and after staring at his shoes for several seconds, asked, "Yeah?"

"What's your name?" he asked.

"What's yours?" she asked.

"I'm Lance Pouliot, Mattawooptock Code Enforcement Officer."

She snorted and lay back down.

"Do you live here?" he asked.

"My family is on vacation," she responded, her nose in the book. "This is our vacation resort."

"Hi kids," he said.

They ignored him. *Dirty little runts.*

"What are you playing?"

Still nothing. They wouldn't even look up from their blocks. No respect.

"Ma'am," he said, returning his attention to the mother, "can you tell me where I might find everybody else?"

"Nope."

Wow, a regular Chatty Cathy, this one. He gave up then and headed farther down the hall. He found three women sitting around a dresser, playing cards. "Hello ladies," he said. It appeared they were betting Goldfish crackers. *Even when they don't have any money, they can't resist gambling.*

Only one of them looked up. "Hi," she said.

"What's your name?" he asked.

"Maggie."

Chapter 10

"Hi, Maggie," the mysterious man with an ominous looking clipboard said. "Do you live here?"

His accusatory tone reminded her of Kirk, and she suddenly wished the floor would open up and swallow her. She looked at her roommates. Jackie, still staring at her cards, subtly shook her head.

"Not really," Maggie answered.

"What does that mean?" he asked.

Her annoyance outgrew her fear. "It means, I don't really live here."

He took a step into the room, which terrified her. She felt herself start to physically shake, and tried to will herself to stop. "Aha," he said. "Well, can you tell me where everyone else is? It's like a ghost town around here."

She didn't know what to say. Her instinct was to lie, but she'd been trying to give that up. But what was the truth, exactly? That Pastor Dan had loaded up the world's oldest school bus with the world's oddest assortment of field-trippers? "Um, I'm not sure exactly where they are at the moment." A pang of guilt hit her, and she tried to smash it down. She concentrated on maintaining eye contact. She thought that would make her look tougher. Homeless people are tough, right?

Without another word, the man with the shiny shoes turned and left, and for the first time, she noticed Cari standing behind him. Cari gave her a huge smile, and Maggie returned it.

Maggie waited several seconds before asking, "Who on earth was that?"

Jackie sighed, "Some code guy. Wants to shut us down."

"Why?" Maggie asked.

Jackie looked at her as if she was stupid. "Why do you think?"

Harmony gave Jackie a dirty look and answered Maggie, "'Cause people hate homeless people."

"Oh," Maggie said, thoughtlessly eating a few of her poker chips. They continued to play, but she was scanning her brain to see if she had ever hated a homeless person. She didn't think she had. Sure, she'd been annoyed when people stopped her on the street to ask for money, but she didn't hate them. She mostly just felt sorry for them, and maybe a little afraid. And, she suddenly realized, she had always thought she was better than them. "He thinks he's better than us." She meant it as a question, but it came out flat like a statement.

"Yep," Jackie said, and laid down a full house.

Chapter 11
Galen

Galen loved the Lord, but he couldn't believe Pastor did this full-time. This was exhausting. He had told everybody to meet back at the mall entrance by one. This had only given them a few hours in the mall, which apparently was plenty of time to cause problems. Galen had spent 20 of those 120 minutes talking with the police. Someone he didn't know, named Rocky, had decided to shoplift some cigarettes. Of course, this was brilliant because he had such a speedy getaway vehicle. And Rocky was a terrible thief. The cashier had seen him take the cigarettes, the police found the smokes in his pocket, and he had been caught on camera. Yet he still insisted he was innocent. As he was finally taken away in cuffs, Pastor Dan promised to go visit him in jail. *Unreal.*

At one o'clock, there were only 20 people at the mall entrance. Galen was irate with himself for not taking a head count before they got off the bus. He was really bad at this. Now here he was, wandering around the mall, looking for people he might not even recognize.

Of course, he found four guys in Spencer Gifts.

He found another in Victoria's Secret, shopping for his girlfriend. He apologized, had lost track of time. It's not like he owned a watch or phone.

He found the woman with the walker testing perfumes at Macy's. The woman behind the counter looked positively exhausted, and silently mouthed "Thank you" when Galen guided walker lady away. She smelled like a perfume factory, and Galen sneezed six times as he walked her toward the door.

When they were almost there, she stopped at a kiosk of tourist fliers. He tried to be patient as she took one of each, but then he lost his patience when she paused to peruse a Fort

Knox brochure. Evidently, that one was special, as she took two more.

That second, he got a text from Pastor Dan: "Entrance. We're leaving."

"Come on, let's go," he said, with a little more snip than he'd intended.

She grabbed the rest of the Fort Knox brochures and followed him, with painful slowness, toward the door. Several hours later, they got there.

"Is this everyone?" Galen asked.

"Don't know," Pastor said, "but if anyone else is here, they're getting left. Plus, we're coming right back, right?"

"Oh yeah," Galen groaned.

They loaded up the bus and headed west. Galen managed to fall asleep. Of course, he dreamed about Maggie. He dreamed that he was kissing her, but when he opened his eyes mid-kiss, he found he was really kissing Eddie. He woke up, slightly terrified, and rubbed his neck. His forehead was frozen from where it had been resting on the window. They were almost home.

The second time around, Galen was much smarter. He counted heads six times, even though there were only 16 people on this trip. Pastor graciously offered to let Galen bow out of this one, but of course, Galen didn't want to. He wanted to go to the mall with Maggie.

He took the seat in front of her on the bus and sat sideways so he could look at her.

"So," he said, "did you meet the code guy?"

"Yes," she said, rolling her beautiful eyes, "he's a tool. Are we really in trouble? The church, I mean."

"Oh probably," Galen said, dropping his gaze to adjust his pant leg, which did not need adjusting. "People are coming to Christ in droves, so of course the enemy wants to shut us down."

"So, what's the deal? What are we doing wrong, though? Are we breaking laws?"

"I don't think so. My understanding is that there are no church codes in Mattawooptock. There are, however, apparently, rules about homeless shelters. Which is strange. Makes me think we just cut and pasted some other real city's rules. Once a shelter gets so big, it needs to meet all sorts of standards. Makes sense, you know? It's better that homeless people sleep on the streets than suffer through a high person to toilet ratio."

Maggie laughed, and it sounded like heaven. "Is that a real thing?"

"I think so," he said, "unfortunately. But I'm not really worried. God will get us through this somehow. He's not going to let some pencil-necked pencil pusher shut us down."

"So, do I really need to spend the money you just handed out, or can I save it?" she asked.

"You can do whatever you want with it," Galen said.

She nodded and looked thoughtful. He wondered what she was thinking. "So how's Eddie?" she asked.

"Good, good," Galen said. "He slept on my pillow again last night. Though he's probably not very happy with me right now. He's been home alone for quite a while now."

"Uh-oh, you may have a little present to come home to then," she said, smirking.

He didn't respond to that, just sat there thinking about all the places Eddie could potentially poop, and hoping for the bathtub, not his laundry basket.

Several minutes passed, and then she asked, "You're not still going to try to deliver the car today, are you?"

"Probably not. I mean, I could go tonight if you're worried about it, or I could go first thing tomorrow."

"Thank you, morning would be great. I doubt he's even worried yet. I'm sure he thinks I'll come crawling back any minute."

Galen had no idea what to say to that so he fell silent again, leaning his head back on the cold, vibrating glass.

This leg of the trip seemed much shorter than the last, and the troupe agreed to meet back at the mall entrance at six. The mall was even busier than it had been in the afternoon, and Galen was suddenly annoyed with the Christmas season. They were playing a rather jovial version of "Grandma Got Run Over by a Reindeer," which didn't help any.

Maggie smiled up at him. "So, I've never been here before. Where's the best place to go if you don't have much money?"

Galen shrugged. "We could get pedicures." She laughed again. He marveled at how funny she thought he was. He really wasn't that funny. At least, no one else had ever thought so. Certainly not his ex-wife.

She nodded at a bench. "You want to just sit and people watch?" she asked. "Unless there was someplace you did want to go?"

He nodded and headed toward the bench. They both sat down, and he asked, "So what are we watching people for?"

She laughed again. "You'll know it when you see it. We just watch. And observe. And comment when necessary. It's like poor man's television."

"Aha," he said, as if he understood, even though he didn't. They sat there for a few minutes, silently watching people. An Amish family walked by, and Galen said, "Amish people go to the mall?"

"See?" she giggled. "You're learning!" She was quiet for a moment, and then she said, "I think it would be fun to be Amish."

And for reasons that he will never be able to explain, Galen chose to say, "I don't know. Their dolls have no faces. That kind of freaks me out." Then he immediately wished he could die.

But Maggie didn't even act as if that was a weird thing to say, which it absolutely was. She just laughed. Then suddenly, she looked up at him. "Would you like an ice cream?"

Galen raised his eyebrows, surprised. "Sure," he said. Like he could say no to Maggie. Or ice cream.

"Let's go," she said, getting up. "I'm buying ... or rather, the church is buying."

Galen wasn't comfortable letting her — or the church — buy his ice cream, but the determined look on her face said it was important.

Maggie dropped her change in the tip bucket and took a sip of her frozen hot chocolate. He wasn't sure how such a thing was even possible; *wouldn't that just be room temperature chocolate?* He took a sip of his caramel cheesecake shake. *Good grief, is that ever delicious! If that's not a fat pill, I don't know what is.*

She started to wander, and he followed.

She pointed at Yankee Candle. "We could use a few of those at the shelter ... I mean church."

"Ayuh," Galen agreed. "A few dozen maybe."

They kept walking.

She nodded toward Hollister. "Ever been in there?"

"Uh, not even close," he said. "I buy my clothes at K-Mart."

She laughed again. "Well, good. Every time I go in there, I feel like I'm going to have a seizure."

They reached the end of the line, and Galen nodded toward Star Nails, "Are you sure, no pedicure?"

She smiled, "I'm sure."

Rather than venture into JCPenney, they turned and headed back the way they had come.

Maggie plopped down on their bench, and crossed her legs. He assumed that she had resumed her people watching, so he joined her. This was the best date he'd ever been on, even if it wasn't a date.

Chapter 12

Maggie was surprised at how glad she was to be back at the church. The mall excursion had been fun, but stepping back into the church felt a lot like coming home. Even though she hadn't seen Eddie all day (Galen had offered to arrange a visit, but Maggie thought he had done enough good deeds for the day), she still felt strangely at ease. The second round of shoppers had missed Bible study, and the attendees were just filing out of the sanctuary. Maggie fell into step with Harmony, and they went to their room.

Maggie was changing into her pajamas when she noticed that Harmony had a bath towel. "Hey, you wouldn't happen to have an extra bath towel, would you?"

"No, this one isn't even mine. I'll go get you one though. Do you need anything else? Toothbrush? Soap?"

Maggie wrinkled her brow, "Why is there like a commissary somewhere?"

Harmony scowled, hanging on the doorframe with one arm, "I don't know what that means, but there's a bunch of stuff in the office people drop off. I can ask for something if you need it."

"Oh! Um, no, just a towel, thanks," Maggie said, though it was a relief to hear there were extra toothbrushes hanging around. She thought about sneaking around on Christmas Eve and sticking them into people's stockings.

Maggie's peripheral vision caught movement in the doorway, and she turned, expecting to see Harmony again, but the person in the doorway wasn't Harmony. She was a short, plump woman, who looked to be about 40, leaning on a walker. "Hi," she said. "I'm your new roomie. My name is Gertrude." Gertrude walked into the room and sat down on Harmony's bed.

"Hi," Maggie said.

"Yep, got kicked out of my apartment. Got to find a new one."

"Oh, well, I'm sorry to hear that. Welcome," Maggie said, and went back to getting ready for bed.

"Why'd you get kicked out?" Jackie asked.

"Well, I'm a collector. I collect things. Or things collect me, not sure which. Ha! And I guess my collections got too big, because they were making my floors bend. So they kicked me out."

"Huh," Jackie said, sounding more interested. "So what happened to your collections?"

Gertrude was silent.

"Hey," Jackie said, snapping her fingers, "what happened to your junk?"

"Jackie!" Maggie scolded.

"What?" Jackie said defensively. "I'm just trying to get to know our new 'roomie.'"

"Well, she just got here. Let's not pummel her with questions. Let's let her relax, OK?"

Jackie rolled her eyes at Maggie, but she stopped interrogating Gertrude. Gertrude lay down on Harmony's bed.

"Um, that bed is taken, Gertrude. The top bunk is open though," Maggie tried.

"Can't get to the top bunk. Can't you see I'm disabled?"

Before Maggie could resolve the issue, Harmony returned. Without so much as a glance at Maggie, Harmony slammed the towel into her chest. "Hey!" she hollered at Gertrude. "That's my bed!"

"It's OK, Harmony," Maggie tried. "She just got here. She didn't know. And she is disabled and can't get up on the top bunk."

"Disabled? That's bull!" Harmony hollered, and kicked Gertrude's walker out of the way.

"Harmony!" Maggie shrieked. What on earth was going on here? Suddenly she understood why Harmony's name didn't always fit.

"Get off my bed before I take you off it!"

Gertrude didn't budge. "I am disabled. I need the bottom bunk."

"So find a different bottom bunk!" Harmony said, and actually grabbed Gertrude by one of her legs and started to pull.

"Harmony, no!" Maggie shrieked again. "You'll hurt her! Calm down, we can figure this out!" Harmony kept pulling, but Gertrude was no lightweight. Harmony started swearing at them both, and Gertrude started making a sound somewhere between giggling and gurgling.

Maggie was downright scared, and was just about to run from the room when a voice behind her said, "Stop." It wasn't loud, but it was definitive. Harmony stopped, and the three of them turned to see that Jackie had stood up. In one fell swoop, she scooped up all her bedding in her arms. "Gert, take my bunk," she said, and threw all her stuff onto the bunk over Harmony's.

Gertrude grunted getting up. Jackie quickly tore the fresh sheets off the top bunk and threw them on Gertrude's new bed. Then she got busy making her own bed. Gertrude just stood there, without her walker, staring at the bed. Harmony stood rooted to her spot, giving Gertrude the death stare. Maggie walked across the room and retrieved Gertrude's walker. She handed it to her, and Gertrude thanked her.

"Want some help making your bed?" Maggie asked.

"Sure," Gertrude said, and then stood still while Maggie completed the chore.

Finally, Harmony sat down on her reclaimed real estate and pulled a bag out from under the bed.

Maggie saw she had a box of hair bleach in her hands. "Careful with that stuff, you can totally fry your hair," she said, trying to lighten the mood.

"Oh what would you know?" Harmony snapped. "You a beautician all of a sudden?"

"No, I went to beauty school, but I never did anything with it," she said, not looking at Harmony.

"Seriously?" Harmony sat stock still, staring at Maggie as if she'd just announced she could turn water to wine. "Will you do this for me? I always do it myself, but I always miss spots."

Maggie laughed. "Me doing it for you won't make the chemicals kinder."

"I know, but … please?"

"Sure, why not?" Maggie sighed. What else did she have to do?

"Can you cut my hair too?"

Maggie didn't want to cut her hair. She hadn't been good at it back when she practiced every day. Now she'd be even worse. She'd give Harmony a disastrous haircut and then Harmony would break her face. She could see it all happening.

"Well?" Harmony asked expectantly.

"Um, I would, but I don't have any scissors."

"I'll go find some," Harmony said, getting up.

"No, they would have to be really sharp. Like hair cutting shears, not like something kids use to cut gluey construction paper."

"I'll go find some," Harmony repeated, and she was gone.

Maggie looked at Jackie, hoping that she would offer some sage advice, but she appeared to have missed the entire interaction. Maggie was still thinking of an escape plan when Harmony returned, carrying two pairs of scissors, each of which had definitely been used to cut gluey construction paper. One was actually a pair of safety scissors, with rounded tips. Maggie was happy about this. Harmony might not be able to stab her with those. The other pair was left-handed and rusty. She didn't want to get stabbed with those.

"OK," Maggie said, taking the scissors. "But you want to dye your hair first, right?" Maggie figured if she took an exceptionally long time with the bleach, maybe Harmony would be too tired for a haircut. Then tomorrow she could make sure to get rid of every pair of scissors in the building.

Chapter 13
Galen

He'd gotten a good night's sleep, but now he just couldn't stop sneezing. He'd already taken a Zyrtec, but it didn't seem to be doing anything. He knew a few Benadryl would squash his allergies, but he had to drive to Massachusetts and back today and he didn't want to fall asleep at the wheel. He grabbed the bottle just in case things didn't improve.

He groaned when he walked through his garage. He hadn't exactly been sitting around twiddling his thumbs lately, but he hadn't done any actual paying work either. He vowed, *tomorrow I will stay away from church (and Maggie) and do some actual work.*

Minutes later, he pulled into the church parking lot and hooked up to Maggie's car again. Then he headed inside. He found her walking to breakfast with another woman. As he said good morning, he realized the other woman was Harmony.

"Whoa, Harmony," he said, "your hair looks great. I didn't even recognize you."

"Thanks. Maggie did it," Harmony said.

So much for no skillset. "Well," he said, "you look nice." Then he turned his attention to Maggie. "Can I borrow you for a sec?"

"Sure," she said, and Harmony headed on to breakfast without her.

"So I've hooked up your car, and I printed out this form here. I'm going to ask him to sign it, so that he can't say he didn't get the car back. Do you think he'll be home, or should I drop it at his workplace?"

"Um … he'll probably be at the office when you get there. Or at least he won't be home. I'm sorry, I don't mean to make you run all over town."

"No worries. I do need an address though, or two addresses, unless of course," Galen took a deep breath, "you just want to ride along and show me where to go?"

She didn't even hesitate. "No, I can't. I can't see him. That would be bad."

Galen was ready for this though. "You don't have to see him. I'll drop you off at Dunkin' Donuts, go take care of business, and then come pick you up." She just stood there, looking at him. "Plus, then you get to snuggle Eddie all day," he added, hoping he didn't sound like he was begging.

Her face lit up at that. "OK, let's do it," she said. "Thanks, Galen."

Of course, Eddie was thrilled to see her.

Of course, Galen had a sneezing fit as soon as he climbed in the cab.

"Are you getting sick?" Maggie asked.

Now here was a dilemma. Admit he was allergic to her little pal, or have her think he was contagious. "No, I think I'm a little allergic to Eddie."

"Oh no," she exclaimed with more alarm than he had anticipated. "I'm so sorry!"

"It's OK, really," he hurried, "I'm medicated. It's all good." He fished the Benadryl out of his pocket and popped one. "It makes me a little sleepy though, so you'll have to entertain me."

She laughed. "I don't know how entertaining I will be. I'm pretty exhausted myself. I was up all night playing salon."

"Oh yeah? She looked great though."

"Well, I was really concentrating 'cause I thought she was going to beat me up. It did come out pretty good, but I think there was luck involved. Some of it came back to me as I went, but mostly I didn't know what I was doing."

"Well, I'm sure the price was right."

"Free is good, but then as soon as I was done, and it took me till like midnight, Gertrude demanded that I cut hers too. So I was up till like 2 a.m., hanging out in the bathroom."

"Gertrude?"

"She's our new roomie, and she's a little … different. She stayed up all night playing with tourist fliers."

"Oh, *Gertrude!*"

They rode along in silence for a while, except for the occasional sneeze and "God bless you" reflex. While the quiet was comfortable, he was pretty drowsy, so he tried to think of something to say that would start a conversation. He failed.

"You mind a little music?"

"No, that would be great," she answered. "Do you mind Christian music though? The other stuff is all about romance, kind of makes me sick."

Well isn't that encouraging? "You got it," he said, and pressed the memory button that would tune his truck to Air 1. Immediately, John Cooper started screaming at them both.

Maggie looked alarmed. "What is this?"

He laughed. "This is Skillet. You know them?"

"I guess not. I'm kind of new to this whole Christian music stuff. I'm kind of new to this whole Christian thing altogether. I only got saved about three months ago."

"Gotcha. Well, Skillet is like the heavy metal of Gospel music. They've been around a long time. Despite all the screaming, they're actually quite talented. They've had a lot of crossover hits and have directed a lot of people, especially teenagers, toward the cross…. I can change it though."

"No, it's cool. I don't mind expanding my boundaries."

He nodded. Eventually, the Skillet gave way to Disciple.

She raised an eyebrow. "Still Skillet?"

"No, but close. This is Disciple."

"Huh. So I guess there's all kinds of headbanging Jesus freaks out there, huh?"

"Yep."

After a few minutes, she said, "I can't understand a word they're saying."

He laughed. "Yeah, it's kind of a skill. The more you listen to them, the easier it gets."

"OK, I'll take your word for it."

"Uh-huh … So, how long have you had Eddie?" he asked, trying to keep the talking going.

"Almost three years," she said, kissing him on the snout. "Kirk got him for me when he was just a puppy. I was home alone all the time, and I would complain about being bored and lonely. I meant that I wanted more time from Kirk, but he got me a puppy instead. At the time, I was mad that he had kind of missed my point, but looking back, I'm really glad he did."

"He worked a lot?"

"Yep. He's a criminal lawyer. A good one. He works a lot and never comes home. At least, he didn't when I was there."

"Sorry."

"Oh, it's OK. That loneliness eventually led me to Jesus, so it's all good."

"Led you to Jesus?"

She giggled, "Well, you know those really annoying people who come to your door to sell you Jesus?"

"Yeah?"

"Well, I was so lonely that I was excited to see them! I invited them right in, and they led me to the Lord. And then Amanda, she was one of them, she kept coming back to see me and disciple me. We became really good friends."

"Oh, wow … so does she know where you are now?"

"Nope. She and her family moved to Africa. They're going door to door there now, I suppose," she said, sounding heartbroken.

"So, is that why you left? Because you lost her?"

Maggie looked at him then, and he could almost feel the weight of what she was about to say. "You promise you won't laugh?"

"Of course not," he said, glad she had warned him in case she was about to say something really nutty.

"Well, this is kind of crazy. I wouldn't believe it if it hadn't happened to me. But I was lying in bed, crying, missing Amanda and basically begging God to do something. I felt like I couldn't survive one more day of my life. I was reading in the Bible, and it kept talking about God rescuing people, and I was like 'Rescue me, God! What about me?' and then I felt him say, clear as day, *clearer* than day actually, 'Go.' That was it—just *go*. He didn't tell me where. I just knew I was supposed to go. So I packed up a few things and I left. I didn't leave a note or anything. I just left. I was filled with an urgent fear, like if I didn't get out of there, the house was going to explode or something, you know?"

Yep. That was kind of crazy, and yet he didn't doubt a word of it. "I think I understand. I've never had God talk to me like that, but I have heard of it happening to other people.... And you're happy? I mean, you're glad he got you out of there?"

"Definitely. I mean, I don't really want to live at a homeless shelter either, but at least I'm safe now," she said, her voice cracking a little.

He wanted to push, but he didn't. He really hoped he wasn't about to come face to face with someone who had hit Maggie. He didn't know if he could handle that.

He went to the house first. Though he didn't know if he should even call it a house. This place didn't even look real. A long, paved, circular driveway led to a house big enough to need four chimneys. *Maggie used to* live *here?* Marveling at the perfectly trimmed hedges sticking out of the snow, he rang the doorbell. No one answered. He waited a minute, and then turned back to his truck.

His GPS led him to the law office building, which was only slightly less impressive than Kirk's home. A neatly dressed woman pressed a button on a futuristic-looking phone and told Mr. Moraski that someone was there to see him. After a few minutes, Galen stood face-to-face with Kirk. And while Galen wasn't too confident in his ability to judge the attractiveness of other men, he could tell this guy was handsome. He kind of looked like a life-sized Ken doll.

"Can I help you?" Kirk asked.

"Yes, I have your car outside. Here," he said, handing him the keys, "and I need a signature of receipt," he said, handing him a clipboard.

Kirk's face was deadpan, but his voice betrayed some emotion. It almost sounded like worry. "Where did you find the car?"

"I can't say," Galen replied.

"Yes, actually, you can. It's my car, and I'm asking you where you got it. There is no tow-truck driver-operator privilege," he said, with more condescension than Galen thought possible.

"OK then," Galen said, annoyed, "then I *won't* say. Do you want the car or not?"

Kirk just stared at Galen, his eyes two miniature icebergs. "I'm not signing that piece of paper until you tell me where you got the car."

"OK then," Galen said. He removed the form from his clipboard and set it on the counter in front of the nice woman with the fancy phone. "Have a nice day."

As he walked away, Kirk said, "I can involve law enforcement if I need to."

Galen didn't respond.

Chapter 14

Maggie didn't ask how the interaction had gone, and Galen didn't say. All she knew was her car was no longer hooked to the back of the tow truck, and for that she was glad. She had left her iPhone and all Kirk's plastic in the glove box, so she was finally untethered.

They got back to church just as Bible study was starting.

"I'd better get in there," Maggie said. "Don't want to get kicked out of my new home."

Galen smiled, but it looked forced. "Mind if I join you?" he asked.

"Of course not," she frowned. As if she would say yes to that.

They walked into the church together and they were barely inside the door before they were accosted by Gertrude. "Are you G?" she asked accusingly.

"Galen, this is Gertrude. Gertrude, Galen."

"We've met," Galen said to Maggie. "Yes, I'm G," he said to Gertrude.

"You have to go get my cats," Gertrude said.

Galen let out a short laugh. Maggie didn't. She was too scared. "I'm sorry?" Galen said.

"My cats. You have to go get them. They are scared."

"OK, well, I'm not really sure why you need me to go get them?" Galen said, and Maggie couldn't believe how sweet he was being to this woman.

Gertrude looked from Galen to Maggie and back to Galen. She looked incredibly confused. "They told me you watched animals for people, 'cause they won't let them in here."

Maggie heard Galen groan, and her own stomach turned. She had done this. This was her fault. "Galen is allergic to cats," Maggie said, trying to help.

"How many cats are there?" Galen asked. Maggie couldn't believe her ears. *Is he crazy?*

"Only five," Gertrude answered.

"Only five," Galen repeated. "OK, and where are they?"

"I don't know," Gertrude said.

"OK," Galen said, and then stood there looking stumped.

"Well, where did you last see them?" Maggie asked. She thought she heard Galen try to squash a laugh. The worship team had fired up and was making it difficult to hear anything.

"At my apartment," Gertrude practically yelled. "But I was arrested, and I had to leave my cats there. You have to find them!"

Galen took a step backward, presumably to distance himself from the speakers. The two women followed. "Why were you arrested?" Galen asked.

Gertrude rolled her eyes as if that were a stupid question, "Because of the cats!"

"Your cats got you arrested?" Galen asked, and Maggie wondered how he was keeping a straight face. She also wondered why he was even still having this conversation.

"Yes," Gertrude said.

"OK, well, what was the arresting officer's name?" Galen asked.

"I don't know."

"Didn't he tell you his name?"

"It was a she."

"OK," Galen sighed, "did *she* tell you her name?"

"No."

"I see. Well, did someone bail you out of jail?"

"I didn't go to jail."

"You got arrested, but you didn't go to jail?" Galen asked, still not seeming frustrated. Maggie couldn't believe it.

"No, she brought me here."

"Oh!" Galen exclaimed as if he suddenly understood everything. "So you weren't really arrested, you were just brought here, right?"

"They didn't ask nicely," Gertrude responded.

"OK. Well, tell you what. I'm not making any promises, but I'll look into it. OK?" Galen asked.

Gertrude didn't say anything. She just nodded, and then spun her walker around and headed into the sanctuary. Maggie looked at Galen, wide-eyed. She was pretty sure her mouth was hanging open too. "Are you an angel?"

He laughed.

"No really? Are you an angel?"

"Hardly," he said, and followed Gertrude into the sanctuary.

Bible study was short, and there was no altar call. The little boy who always goes down front looked disappointed. Once they were dismissed, she walked to the door with Galen.

"Well, good night," he said, and it sounded a little awkward.

"Yeah, good night. And really, Galen, thanks again. Maybe you're an angel, and you just don't know it," she said. She had a strong urge to hug him, but she didn't. She wasn't sure why. She was just afraid.

He smiled, "Not an angel. Trust me. Good night. Don't let them keep you up all night playing salon."

"I won't," she said, and he was gone. She missed him already.

She hadn't even gotten back to her room before she was approached by a woman she didn't know. "I hear you're giving haircuts?" she asked.

"Well, sort of. I'm not licensed or anything. I can't do anything fancy. What do you need?"

She pointed at her head. "Anything but this? I haven't had a real haircut in years."

"Yeah, well, OK. Give me a few minutes and then I'll meet you in the bathroom by the stairs."

"OK," she said, and headed that way.

Maggie went to her room to get her comb, scissors, towel, and shampoo. As soon as she stepped into the room, Gertrude said, "Your boyfriend is nice."

"He's not my boyfriend," Maggie quickly said.

"Why not?" Gertrude asked. "He has fabulous buttocks."

Maggie didn't respond. She fled instead, suddenly very grateful that she had opened a salon in the bathroom.

The woman was there waiting for her, already sitting in the rusty folding chair Maggie had dragged into the bathroom the night before. "Hi!" Maggie said brightly. "What's your name again?"

"Delores."

"OK Delores, do you want to start with a shampoo?"

"Yes, please."

"Alrighty then. I've been asking people to stand for that part, and bend over the sink. Sorry, I know it's not very comfortable, but it's the only way I can figure out how to get all the hair wet, without getting you all wet too."

"No problem," Delores said, and bent over the sink.

Maggie turned the water on and let it heat up. "Let me know if it's too hot or cold," she said, as she used a cup to pour water over Delores's head.

"OK," Delores mumbled.

It was obvious Delores hadn't had a haircut in a while. Maggie also got the impression she hadn't had a shampoo in a while. She scrubbed vigorously for a few minutes and then rinsed. "Sorry, I don't have any conditioner," Maggie said, as she wrapped a towel around Delores's head.

"No problem, neither do I," Delores said, standing up. "Thank you, by the way."

"Yeah, sure," Maggie said, "have a seat."

Delores sat.

Maggie towel dried her hair and then began to try to comb out the ends. *This is going to take forever*, she thought. "So, any idea what you want for a cut? I'm not sure I can do it, but I can try."

"Nope," Delores said. "I just want it shorter, so it will be easier to take care of."

"OK great," Maggie said, setting down the comb. "I'm going to cut some of it off first then. That will make it easier to comb out. And then I'll straighten things up after."

"OK," Delores said, and Maggie marveled at how trusting she was. Maggie began to cut. Giant chunks of dark brown hair fell to the floor. Delores looked down. "Wow," she said.

"So, where are you from Delores?" Maggie asked.

"Connecticut originally. But last place I was in was Commack. Had a boyfriend there. But he got arrested, so I hitched here."

"Ah, I see," Maggie said. "Are you going to stay here till he gets out?"

Delores laughed, "No way. Guy was a total, well, he was a thing I can't say in church. Plus, he's going to be in for a long time."

"Oh," Maggie said. She wanted to ask what he went to prison for, but she bit her lip.

"He sold pills," Delores told her anyway. "Got caught with a whole bunch of 'em."

"Oh," Maggie said again. She couldn't think of anything else to say.

The bathroom door opened then, and two women came in. One of them said, "You got time for another dye?" She held up a box. "I got this today for ya."

Maggie didn't really agree that the woman had purchased the box *for her*, but she just nodded and accepted the fact that she was going to be up for a while. "You too?" she said, looking at the other woman.

"No," the woman said as if that was ridiculous. "I'm just here to watch."

"Don't worry, Allie," Delores said. "Maggie knows what she's doing."

Maggie wasn't sure how Delores could tell that yet, but she accepted the compliment. "So, which one of you is Allie?"

"Me," said the woman by the door.

The other one hopped up onto the register. "I'm Janelle," she said.

"Janelle!" Delores exclaimed. "Isn't that hot?"

"Yep," Janelle concurred. "It feels good on my bum," she said, drawing out the "m" on the end of bum far longer than necessary. All the women cackled. "You don't charge anything, do you?" Janelle asked.

"Nope, couldn't if I wanted to. I don't have a license."

"You don't have a license? Then what are you doing cutting hair?" Janelle asked, sounding horrified.

Maggie sighed. "I don't know. People just keep showing up," she said, not looking up from Delores's head.

"You should make a sign," Janelle said.

"What?" Maggie asked.

"You know, like real hairdressers have their licenses on the wall. You should hang a sign that says 'not licensed.'"

Maggie stopped cutting. "You want me to hang a sign in the women's bathroom?"

"Why not?" Janelle argued.

"OK. You make me a sign, I'll hang it."

Janelle was back in about two minutes with a piece of tape and a piece of paper that said in black marker: "Warning. Not Licensed." Janelle hung it up over the tampon dispenser as if she was doing a tremendous public service. "There," she said, hands on her hips and staring at her finished product.

It took some time, but Maggie managed to get Delores's ends even while the rest of the women discussed the men in the shelter. Maggie heard some things she wished she could unhear. "OK, keep it clean," she said. "No bedroom talk in my salon!" They all laughed at that, which made Maggie feel as if this was actually her place: this weird little bathroom in the weird church in the town with the weird name.

Chapter 15

Maggie woke up the next morning to pounding on her door. She tried to ignore it, but the pounder was persistent. She looked around the room and found that she was alone. This was odd. Jackie rarely left the room. She got up and groggily opened the door to find six smiling faces positively gleaming at her. One of them was Harmony.

"What?" she asked, a little abruptly, but she had never seen so many smiles at once—it frightened her.

"We all pitched in," Harmony said, "and got you a present." A girl she recognized, but didn't really know, held out a small item loosely wrapped in crinkled tissue paper.

"Thanks?" Maggie said, gingerly taking it. She unwrapped it to find a brand new, shiny pair of cutting shears. They were beautiful, iridescent silver—they appeared to be covered in rainbows. Despite herself, Maggie teared up. "I … I don't know what to say," she said. The girls were all still smiling, obviously quite proud of themselves.

"Don't say anything," one of them said, "just cut our hair."

"OK," Maggie said, and laughed. But the one who had said it was still looking at her as if she was expecting something else. "Like right now?" Maggie asked.

"Yes!" the girl exclaimed.

"Um, what time is it?" Maggie asked.

"Almost lunchtime, you sleepyhead," Harmony answered.

"How about after lunch?" Maggie asked. "I'll take a shower and eat and then anyone who wants to can help me break these in?"

They all said yes and turned to go. Maggie shut the door and turned around to lean on it. *Well,* she thought, *I still don't know what I'm doing, but at least I've got sharp scissors now.*

Maggie showered, dressed, and then went to lunch. She felt different, better than she had in a long time, maybe ever. She didn't know where it was coming from, but she felt energetic and more alive than usual. On her way back from lunch, she had to pass by the bathroom on her way to her room. Three women were lined up at the door.

"I'll be right back," Maggie said. "I just have to go get some supplies. And if any of you want a shampoo, you'll have to bring me some. I'm all out."

As she was walking away, she heard one of them say, "But I don't want to lose my place in line!"

Maggie grabbed her stuff and returned to the bathroom. The women followed her in. "You should set up some chairs for a waiting room," one of them said. Maggie couldn't tell whether she was kidding.

"So who's first?" Maggie asked, and one of them immediately plopped down in the chair. "OK, and what's your name again?"

"Clarissa."

"Hi Clarissa, what do you want done?" Maggie asked. Then, to Maggie's horror, Clarissa pulled a folded magazine picture from her pocket. She unfolded it to show thick, lustrous hair that fell around a model's face in wide, bouncy curls of varying lengths. Clarissa's hair was straight as ruler. "Um, I don't know if I can do this?"

"What do you mean?" Clarissa asked.

"I mean, I don't know if it's possible, and if it is, I don't know how to do it."

"But you're a hairdresser! How can you not know how to do it?" Clarissa stood up, her face beet red. "Fine then, I'll just go to a real hairdresser! Screw this place!" And she stormed out.

Maggie stood still, in shock, trying not to cry. But no one else seemed to be in shock. Someone else immediately sat down in the chair. "Don't get upset 'cause of her," the woman said. "She's crazy, and everybody knows it. My name is Kate, and you can do whatever you want to my hair. Just don't make me look like an old lady."

Maggie cut hair all afternoon. Her feet were killing her. But she was more tired from listening to her customers' stories than she was from the actual work. Candy was an 18-year-old fresh out of the foster care system. She'd never lived anywhere for more than a year. Tammy had been in and out of jail. From the way it sounded, she was just waiting to get back in. Alice was an alcoholic—she said nothing to indicate that she was in recovery, just talked about how much alcohol had destroyed her life. Julie didn't say much about how she'd gotten to the church; she just shared a list of diagnoses: PTSD, ADHD, and OCD.

Marissa was a recovering pill addict. When Maggie finished her hair, Marissa stood up and looked in the mirror. She stood there silently for a minute and then began to cry. "That's the best I've looked in a long, long time," she spoke in a near-whisper. "Thank you, Maggie."

As Marissa was leaving, the woman with five kids showed up—with all five of her kids. "I don't think I'll have time to do all of you before dinner," Maggie said.

"Oh, that's OK," the woman hurried to say. "It's just Jake. He wondered if you could give him a haircut."

"Oh sure," Maggie said, "have a seat, Jake." The little boy who went down front for every altar call stepped forward. Maggie smiled at him. He sat down. "So, what would you like me to do?" Maggie asked his mother, as she started to run a comb through his hair. But before the mom could answer, Maggie saw something she didn't want to see. She checked behind his ears, just to make sure, and then said to the mom, "What's your name again?"

"Sarah," she said, seeming to recognize from Maggie's tone that something was wrong.

"Can you come here for a sec, Sarah?" Maggie asked. Sarah walked around to where Maggie stood, and Maggie pointed to what she'd found.

"What is it?" Sarah asked.

"Lice," Maggie mouthed, not wanting to freak the other kids out.

Sarah looked as if she was about to cry.

"It's OK," Maggie whispered, "we can take care of it. Can I check your hair?"

"You don't have to," Sarah said, the tears falling now. "My head is wicked itchy. I just didn't know why. Thought my skin was just dry."

"What's wrong, Mama?" another one of the boys said, coming to her and grabbing her leg.

"OK," Maggie said, thinking quickly. She'd never actually had to deal with lice before, but they had learned about it in school. "Hang on, I'm going to go get help. Don't worry, this is a piece of cake," she said, surprised at her own compassion, but Sarah was really upset.

"Please don't tell anyone."

"I won't," Maggie said. "I'm only going to tell Pastor or Cari, whoever I find first. Just so I can get some supplies. Just stay here and try to relax. I'll be right back."

Maggie left them and practically ran to the office. Cari was there, and Maggie silently thanked God that she was. "Cari, we have a problem."

"OK," Cari said, looking up. "What is it this time?"

"I've got the big family, you know, Sarah's family, in my bathroom, and well, they've got lice. Can you go get some supplies?"

"Oh no, not again," Cari said, turning to get into the safe. "Yep, I'll go get some stuff and bring it to the bathroom. You're going to help them with it?"

"Yes, except that we're also going to have to wash all their clothes and bedding. I'll need some help, but I promised I wouldn't tell anybody except you."

"OK, I have to tell Pastor, but I'll try to keep it on the down low."

Maggie returned to the bathroom. Jake had given up his seat to his mom and was now seated on the floor. One of his siblings was on either side of him, poking through his hair. They took turns exclaiming, "I found one!" The youngest child sat in Sarah's lap, crying silently.

"Is she scared?" Maggie asked.

Sarah nodded.

"Hey," Maggie said softly, tugging on the toddler's pant leg and squatting down to meet his eyes. "Trust me, it's nothing to be scared of. They are just annoying little bugs. They won't hurt you. And we're going to get rid of them, OK?" The toddler stuck a dirty thumb in his mouth and nodded. Maggie smiled.

"Thank you so much," Sarah said to Maggie. "I don't know how you're not grossed out. I certainly am."

"Nah," Maggie said. "It's no trouble, really, though we are probably going to miss dinner. We shouldn't be rubbing shoulders with anyone right now."

"Miss supper?" one of the kids cried, and Maggie regretted saying anything.

"Don't worry!" Maggie exclaimed. "I'll go ask them to set some extra food aside for us. I'll be right back."

Maggie left them and went to the kitchen, which was packed. She found the person who looked most likely to be in charge and said, "Sarah and her family can't make it to dinner right now. Can you set aside some food for them? I can come get it later."

"Can't," the woman said.

"Why?"

"Just can't. Against the rules."

"Whose rules?" Maggie asked.

"Mine."

Maggie didn't know what to say. She'd never encountered anyone so obnoxious in her whole life. Furious, she left the kitchen and went to look for Pastor. He was nowhere to be found. She asked everyone if they'd seen him, and everybody had, but he wasn't in any of the places where he had been sighted. She felt as if she was playing hide and seek with a ghost. Finally, she found Cari in the office, who told her that Pastor had run to the store to get supplies. Maggie explained the kitchen crisis to Cari, who said, "Oh that Rita. Always on a power trip. I'll take care of it."

On her way back to the bathroom, Maggie stopped in the only Sunday school room that was still in fact a Sunday school room and found some crayons and paper. She went back into the bathroom and offered the crayons to the kids. A medium-sized one exclaimed, "Crayons are for babies!"

Sarah snapped, louder than Maggie thought possible, "You will say thank you!"

And the kid said, "Thank you."

They all waited in a restless silence for what seemed like a really long time. Maggie made a mental note to find a clock to hang above her no license sign. That way people could make appointments. She would need a notebook too, to keep track of those appointments. She was just about to leave to find a clock when someone knocked on the bathroom door. Before Maggie could get there, one of the kids hopped up and opened it.

"Thank you," Pastor Dan said and strode into the women's restroom as if he did it all the time, paying no heed to the "no men allowed" sign, which seemed reasonable, as he was probably the one who had written it.

"Here you go," he said, handing Maggie two of the six Walmart bags he carried. He set two more in the corner. "These bags are full of clean clothes for y'all. Once Maggie finishes with you, put them on. Leave yours in a pile on the floor. We'll wash them and get them back to you. Once you're dressed, please go wait in the kitchen. Your supper will be waiting for you. We can't let you get back to your room until we've cleaned it thoroughly, so please be patient."

Huh, Maggie thought. *It's almost as if he's done this before.*

He turned to go, and then paused. "Almost forgot," he said, turning toward Maggie and handing her a bathing cap.

"Thanks," Maggie said. "Do you have any clippers? It'll make the little boys a lot faster."

"They're in one of the bags," he said, without turning around.

As the door shut, Maggie said, "OK then, let's get started." She started with Sarah, to show the kids that it wasn't going to be scary.

"Please, just cut it," Sarah said.

"Are you sure?"

"Absolutely."

So, Maggie washed, cut, and combed out Sarah's hair. She buzzed the four boys, and then went to work on the only girl. As she was combing out her hair, there was another knock on the door. This time he didn't wait for an answer; Pastor opened the door and he had two kids with him. "We've got a couple more. Are you up for it?"

"Yes," Maggie said, even though she wasn't.

"Great, thanks," Pastor said. "And we're still checking everybody else, so stand by."

Maggie suppressed a groan and forced herself to smile at the two little boys. Only one of them had to be talked into a buzz cut. As Maggie finished up the second, Sarah began directing traffic at the door. Another child and two adult men had arrived.

Maggie washed, cut, and combed until three o'clock in the morning. When Pastor finally told her it was a wrap, she washed and combed out herself, just to make sure. Then she fell into her freshly laundered sheets that someone else had put on her bed. She was too tired to eat, too tired to think, too tired to do anything. But she wasn't too tired to notice that she was feeling something pretty special. She wasn't exactly sure what to call it, but she thought maybe it was simply purpose.

Chapter 16

The first thing Maggie thought of in the morning was Eddie. She hadn't even seen him the day before, and she missed him terribly. The second thing she thought of was her bathroom. She vowed that unless there was a louse sighting, she would take the day off.

They didn't make it easy on her. On her way to the office, two people asked her for haircuts. "Talk to me at Bible study," she said. "We'll make an appointment."

Maggie dragged herself into the office. "Good morning," she said to Cari.

"Wow, you look tired," Cari said.

"So do you," Maggie said back.

"I haven't been to bed yet. Still doing laundry," Cari said.

"Oh, wow," Maggie said, "you're a saint."

"We're all saints. What can I do for you? I'm assuming you didn't just come to chat?"

"Right," Maggie said. "I was wondering if you had a notebook I could have, and I was wondering if I can use the phone to call Galen."

"Yes, and yes," Cari said. "I wish all requests were that simple." She handed the phone to Maggie. "You got his number?"

"Yep."

"Of course you do," Cari said, a little too suggestively for Maggie's taste.

Maggie ignored her and dialed the phone.

"Hullo?"

"Hey, it's Maggie. How are you?"

"I'm fine. How are you holding up?"

"I'm good. Hey, I know you're busy, but if there's a way I could see Eddie today, I would be very grateful."

"Yeah, sure," Galen said quickly, "I brought him by yesterday, but then someone warned me at the door about the outbreak, so I ran away." He laughed at his own joke. "Is it safe now?"

"I think so?" she said.

"OK, well, I've got to work today, but if you don't mind hanging out alone with Eddie, I can come pick you up and bring you back here."

"Sure!" Maggie said with obvious excitement.

"Cool, I'll be there in a bit."

"Awesome, thanks so much, Galen."

"You bet. Bye."

"Bye." She hung up the phone and noticed Cari staring at her. Cari handed her the notebook. "Thanks," Maggie said, trying to avoid eye contact.

"He's a good guy, you know," Cari said.

"I know, I'm just … I'm just not ready for anything like that."

"Yeah well, don't wait too long or someone else will scoop him up," she said, and then scurried off, probably back to the laundry room.

True to his word, Galen was at the church within minutes. Maggie ran out and jumped into the truck. She scooped an ecstatic Eddie up into her arms and peppered him with kisses.

"Hi, Galen, it's so nice to see you," Galen said in a high-pitched voice, making fun of Maggie's complete failure to greet the human in the truck.

She laughed. "Sorry. Hi, Galen, it's so nice to see you!" she said with exaggerated sweetness.

"It's OK," he said, putting the truck in drive, "I know where I rank."

A few minutes later, Galen pulled into his garage. As Maggie climbed out of the truck, Eddie started barking ferociously. Maggie looked in the direction of his barks and saw a pyramid of what looked like small dog crates against the opposite wall.

"Are those cats?" she asked, aghast.

He laughed and climbed out of the truck. "Yep, Maggie, Gertrude's cats. Gertrude's cats, meet Maggie. Eddie positively hates them."

As if to accent that fact, Eddie barked again.

"Are you insane?" Maggie asked, and then, without letting him answer, "How did you find them?"

"Oh, it was simple, really," Galen answered. "Cari told me Gertrude was from Winslow. So I called the Animal Control Officer, who, after talking my ear off about how hard her job is, told me which shelter the cats were at. Then, I drove to the animal shelter and asked which cats had been brought in together on the date the Animal Control Officer gave me. And voila! Gertrude's cats."

Maggie shook her head. "You didn't have to *pay* for them, did you?"

"Almost," Galen said. "But when I explained the situation, they let me take them. I had to be persuasive. Even had to flirt."

Maggie's head snapped around. "Flirt?" she asked.

He laughed. "Yep, I turned on the Turney charm."

She realized then that she hadn't known Galen's last name till just now. *Galen Turney. It has a nice ring to it, doesn't it?* She wanted to ask him more about this flirting, but he cut her off.

"So, you and Eddie go make yourself at home if you want. I've got work to do."

Maggie headed upstairs. Eddie followed, barking ferociously over his shoulder at the felines. Once inside, the two of them settled into the sofa, and Maggie started to flip through the channels. This was no small task. It seemed that Galen had at least a thousand of them. She settled on a Lifetime movie, but then had trouble focusing. *Why am I so bothered by the idea of Galen flirting with someone?* she thought. *I don't like him, do I? I mean, not in that way? I'm not attracted to him. I mean, he's not ugly or anything. I guess he's kind of handsome in a way. He does have nice eyes ...* As she was thinking about this, the Lifetime movie launched into a love scene that was more than she could take. She opted for Syfy instead, but within seconds, a curvy woman in a jumpsuit was making out with a green man with horns. *Why is the whole universe obsessed with romance?* she asked herself and then flipped through till she found Animal Planet. Relieved it wasn't a special about dolphin mating rituals, she settled in to watch *Treehouse Masters.* She briefly wondered if Galen would be offended if she put her feet on his couch, and then decided that he wouldn't be. She lay down as if she owned the place, placed Eddie on her chest, and promptly fell asleep.

She woke to Galen shaking her foot.

"Ah, sorry," she said, sitting up suddenly and knocking Eddie onto his back. He flailed his legs for a sec and then jumped down on the floor and gave her a dirty look.

"You don't have anything to be sorry for. I was just going to order some takeout and wondered if you wanted any."

"Oh, yeah, I would love some, but I don't want to be a mooch."

"You're not a mooch," Galen answered, sitting down beside her.

His hands were black, and he smelled like oil. This made her happy. *Do I like him?* she wondered, almost panicking.

"Unless of course you already went through my fridge and ate everything in there."

He was staring at her.

"Huh?" she asked.

He gave her a little scowl. "I said, you're not a mooch unless you've already gone through my fridge."

"Oh, no, I didn't do that."

"Well, obviously. Besides, all that's in there is some orange juice and ketchup. So, where were your thoughts?"

"Oh, nowhere, I guess I'm just not really awake yet."

"OK," he said, looking skeptical, "so Thai food? Chinese? Pizza?"

"Are there really that many choices in Mattawooptock, Maine?"

"There sure are," he said, rubbing his belly. "We Mainers know how to eat."

She laughed. "Sure then, whatever you want. Beggars can't be choosers, right?"

He looked at her, his face serious, "Maggie, you're not a mooch or a beggar. You are my friend, and I'm offering to feed you. I want to bless you with something you enjoy. So you pick. Besides, I hear you've been earning your keep lately."

She smiled. "Thai food. And yes, I've been working, for sure. My feet are killing me. I need one of those squishy mats to stand on."

He fiddled with his phone and came up with a Thai menu. "Here you go," he said, handing her the phone.

"I don't even need to look at it," she said. "Drunken noodles please, extra spicy."

"Oh, you're one of *those*," he said, his eyes twinkling. He hit the dial button and ordered their food.

"So, you've heard about my salon for the homeless, huh?" she asked when he'd hung up.

"I have, and it got me thinking," he stood up and walked over to the counter in his kitchen. He returned with some papers and handed them to her. The top of the front one said, "How to Obtain a Maine Cosmetology License." She looked at him, surprised. He sat back down and continued, "It looks like all you have to do is take two exams and you could be licensed."

"You think I need to be licensed to cut hair for free at a homeless shelter?" she said, with more attitude than she'd intended.

"No," he said quickly. He leaned back on the couch. "Sorry, I was just trying to help. I thought you wanted to find a job."

She felt horrible. She didn't even know why she had reacted that way. "I'm sorry, Galen. No, you're right. This is great information. Thanks."

He nodded, but he didn't look convinced. He looked wounded. "I'm going to go get the food. Do you want to ride along?"

"Sure," she said. She got up and followed him to the door. As they walked down the stairs into the garage, they passed the cats. "Does Gertrude know?" Maggie asked.

"Does Gertrude know what?"

"That you rescued her cats?"

"Oh that, yeah, I left a message for her with Cari, so I assume so."

"I think you're lying," Maggie said, almost flirtatiously. She was trying to make up for snapping at him about the license, but his head whipped around as if she'd said something horrible.

"About what?" he demanded.

"About being an angel."

Chapter 17

Maggie got back to church just before Bible study. Someone had put a crooked Charlie Brown tree in the corner of the sanctuary, and a dozen people were crowded around it. As she approached, she could hear them arguing about how to decorate it. She decided she didn't want to be involved in that, so she veered off toward her room to get her appointment notebook. Cari caught her though, "Good grief, where have you been?"

"Oh no," Maggie groaned, "did we have another outbreak?"

Cari smiled, "No, but people are looking for you. Everyone wants haircuts."

Maggie sighed. "I really thought I had given every woman in this building a haircut by now."

"You may have. These were the men asking."

"Oh no," Maggie said. She felt her heart rate increasing. "I really don't want to be alone in the bathroom with men."

"Good point," Cari said, "let me talk to Pastor, and we'll see if we can come up with a plan." She paused, and then added, "And you speak up if you get sick of this."

"Sick of what?" Maggie asked.

"Sick of being the church beautician. I know you never really volunteered for this."

"Did you volunteer to run the whole homeless shelter?" Maggie asked.

"No, actually," Cari said thoughtfully. "It's just that no one else was doing it."

"Exactly," Maggie said, and headed off to her room.

When she returned to the sanctuary, she was bombarded with appointment requests. She made several for the following day. The service was just about to start when Gertrude asked for another appointment.

"But I just cut your hair," Maggie said.

"I know, but I want a permanent," Gertrude said.

Maggie laughed, "I don't have the supplies do perms, Gertrude. Sorry."

"What's a perm?"

"A permanent. I don't have the supplies to do a permanent."

"Well, when are you going to get them?"

"So, I met your cats!" Maggie tried to change the subject.

"You did? Oh, how are they?" Gertrude grabbed one of Maggie's hands in both of hers and squeezed tightly. "How are they?"

"They're doing great, Gertrude. They are warm, and fed, and safe. I'm sure they miss you, but other than that, they're in great shape."

"Oh goodie. Now I had no idea that young gentleman allowed people to come visit their pets. I'll have to give him a call tomorrow."

Oops, Maggie thought, *I just threw Galen under the bus again, and it's the same bus at that.* But it was too late to take it back. Gertrude slid into the seat beside her and turned her attention to the worship team as they fired up the guitars.

After a few raucous songs, including an amped up version of "It Is Well with My Soul," the Pastor introduced a guest speaker. Chuck had been homeless only 18 months ago. "My life was a train wreck," he shared. "My wife had left me. Taken my kids. And I drank so much, I couldn't keep a job. All I cared about was the booze. All I could think about was the next drink. I didn't really care if I lived or died. But then I found the Lord, right there at that altar," he said, turning around to point at the altar. He was silent for a moment, just staring at it. The congregation was also silent, which was rare. They seemed to be hanging on his every word.

"And," he continued, "everything changed. And I mean everything. My heart changed. I got on the wagon, started going to AA. Pastor helped me find a job, and I got a good one now, working at the grocery store. I even got my wife and kids back. I apologized to my wife, and I've proven myself, and now we're a family again. We've got an apartment in Augusta, and we've found a great church, not as great as this one, but pretty great."

Pastor Dan got up to pray over Chuck, and then Chuck returned to his seat. The place erupted in applause. Pastor talked for a bit more, but it was hard to follow Chuck's act, so the worship team took the stage again for a few more songs.

Pastor concluded the service with an altar call and nine people went down front. Maggie's eyes teared up again. *I should be getting used to this*, she thought. She realized that Jake hadn't joined the people at the altar yet, and she looked around for him, but didn't see him or his mom anywhere.

After the closing prayer, Cari dumped a bag of Christmas ornaments out on the back pew. "Now, no fighting!" she declared as most of the kids, and several adults, dove into the pile to get to work. Cari stood back and watched, smiling.

Maggie walked over to join her. "You're amazing," she said.

Cari laughed, "Nah, not me."

"No really, doing all you do for us, it's amazing."

"Oh, it's no big thing … just a steady stampede of small things," she said, and laughed.

"I guess," Maggie said. "I mean, do you ever go home?"

Cari looked at her then, her face serious, "I am home."

"Oh," Maggie said, embarrassed. "Sorry, I didn't know you were homeless too."

"Nothing to be sorry about, kiddo, and I'm not homeless, not anymore."

Maggie was quiet for a minute, but then she remembered Sarah. "Do you know where Sarah and her kids are?"

"They left."

"What do you mean? Left to go where?"

"I don't know. They just left."

Maggie was struck then with a new kind of grief. It almost took her breath away.

"You OK?" Cari asked.

"Yeah, I just … I just didn't even get a chance to say goodbye."

Cari nodded knowingly, "You'll get used to it. People come and go."

"I don't know if I can get used to that. I really liked her, I mean, we were becoming friends … How long have you been here, Cari?"

"Since the beginning … since Dan first opened the doors."

Chapter 18

Maggie fell into a comfortable routine. She knew she was supposed to be coming up with a plan, but she was beginning to wonder if this *was* the plan. She had learned that her number one priority in life was to seek God, and this was the perfect place to do it.

She woke up every morning with ample time to spend in prayer and in the Word. Then she would head "to work" in her bathroom. She wasn't always busy, but she hadn't yet gone a day without someone needing a trim. A few women had even asked her to wax various parts of their bodies, but so far, she'd managed to avoid those particular business prospects.

She began to crave the evening Bible studies. Every night, she learned something new. Pastor Dan usually led them, but sometimes they had guest speakers, and sometimes other church members filled in. A few of the long-term guests even tried their hand at teaching, though it was difficult to get the back rows quiet during those lessons.

Maggie had lots of questions, but Pastor or Galen was always able to answer them. She was so grateful for, and impressed by, how well Galen knew the Bible. It seemed as though he had an appropriate Scripture for just about any situation. At least, she *thought* he was quoting Scripture. She supposed he could just be making stuff up. But if so, it was convincing.

One Saturday afternoon, she was at Galen's house. He had let her pick out a movie, and she had picked a bad one. She could tell he was irritated.

"Want to watch basketball instead?" she asked.

"Nah, I'm OK thanks."

"Well, I'm not. This movie's terrible."

Galen laughed. "That it is. Sorry, I'm not big on chick flicks. Especially one that portrays the husband as a big, dumb oaf. I don't find man-hating entertainment."

Maggie heard a lot of irritation in his voice, and without thinking asked, "Was your wife a man-hater?"

Galen looked stunned, and Maggie wished she could take it back.

Finally he said, "I don't know, but she was a me-hater." Then, a few seconds later he added, "It's not that I was a bad husband. I really tried to be a good one, but she just wasn't satisfied. She wasn't a believer, and she was annoyed that I was. She wanted more excitement in life. So she left to find it." He shrugged.

"I'm so sorry, Galen," Maggie whispered. She had the urge to slide down the couch and hold his hand, but she didn't want to send any signals. She felt for his pain, but she certainly didn't want to suggest she was volunteering to fill the vacancy.

"Yeah, me too," Galen said, not looking at her. They finished watching the terrible movie in a terrible silence.

When they got in the truck to go back to church, Galen asked, "How did you know I was married?"

"Someone at church mentioned it," she said. "Can I pry a little more?"

"Shoot."

"Why did you marry an unbeliever? I mean, isn't that a no-no?"

Galen snickered. "Well, I didn't, really. We both grew up in the church. Got married at 18, thanks to some raging hormones. Then after a few years, she just sort of lost interest in Jesus, and in me. Claimed she never really believed in the first place. Told me I was a child for still believing. She compared Christ to Santa Claus."

"Oh, Galen," Maggie said, unable to think of anything else to say.

As they pulled into the church parking lot, a crowd distracted them.

"What are they all looking at?" Maggie asked.

"No idea ... let's go see." Galen parked the truck, and he and Maggie walked up to the swelling crowd, many of whom were hollering things toward the center. Soon Maggie was able to see that two men were in the center of the circle, fighting. And it looked as though they'd been fighting a while. They were bruised and bloodied, so it took a second for Maggie to realize they were Hershel and Dale.

Galen didn't even seem to think first. He just ran into the center of the circle and pushed the two men apart. They kept swinging, but Galen's shoulders were broad enough so that any punches that landed did so with an embarrassing lack of oomph.

The two men finally admitted defeat, and Galen let go. Dale bent over and clutched his knees, suddenly caught in a coughing fit. "What on earth is wrong with you two?" Galen shouted. He was obviously mad, but even in anger he seemed completely in control. Maggie wasn't used to this kind of angry.

Neither man would answer him. Galen gave them a minute, and then ordered everyone inside. Maggie was surprised that most people obeyed him. She wasn't sure when they had put him in charge, but it worked.

Galen walked over to her. "I'm late for worship team practice. If you want to do some sleuthing, go find out what that was all about. I'm curious."

Maggie nodded. She was curious too.

Galen headed into the sanctuary, and Maggie went down to get some coffee, knowing it would be terrible. But there was some expired Irish Cream coffee creamer, so that perked things up a bit.

It didn't take much sleuthing. Everybody was talking about the fight. Apparently, Hershel owed Dale five dollars.

Disappointed that the scoop wasn't very juicy, she went to her room. There, Jackie filled her in on the truth: It wasn't really about the money. Hershel had found an apartment. Hershel was leaving. Hershel was leaving Dale.

Chapter 19

About a week before Christmas, Mr. Pouliot showed up at breakfast. He stood in the corner in his suit and shiny shoes and made a theatrical show of doing a headcount.

"Gosh I hate that guy," Jackie mumbled, her mouth full of scrambled eggs.

"Come on, Jackie," Harmony said, "we're supposed to love our enemies."

"Yeah, you're one to talk," Jackie said.

"What's that supposed to mean?" Harmony snapped, slamming her fork down on the table.

Jackie rolled her eyes, "I rest my case."

Maggie laughed, and Jackie's head snapped up, suspicious. But Maggie wasn't laughing at them. She had just seen Gertrude come down the stairs, holding her walker in one hand like an unwieldy suitcase.

Pastor walked over to talk to Mr. Pouliot. Maggie marveled at how calm Pastor seemed. He could have been discussing the weather with an old friend. They talked for quite a while, and then Pastor said something Mr. Pouliot obviously didn't like. His face twisted up in a spasm, and then he turned and headed up the stairs alone. And on his way up, he came face to face with Clarissa, who was on her way down, and she looked *mad*. Maggie's gasp caused Harmony and Jackie's heads to whip around to follow her stare.

"Uh-oh," Harmony said.

Clarissa didn't even seem to notice the man in the suit, but as soon as she saw Pastor, she started to scream. It was hard to understand her, but Maggie made out several naughty words, as well as the word "pills."

Pastor seemed to be trying to reason with her, and didn't seem to be having much success. She was about two inches from his face and still screaming. After a few minutes, he took his phone out of his pocket and called someone.

"I wonder who he's calling," Maggie wondered aloud.

"Cops," Jackie said matter-of-factly.

Maggie looked at Jackie, but it seemed that Jackie had lost interest in the scene. Maggie didn't know how that was possible; Clarissa was so *loud*. "Why, has this happened before?"

"Not that I know of," Jackie said, "but who else would he be calling?"

She had a point. Pastor was on the phone less than a minute, and then he hung up and announced, "I need everyone in the sanctuary right now."

Jackie groaned. Everybody stood up, took a last swig of canned orange juice or coffee, and then obediently headed upstairs. On the way, Maggie saw Gertrude swipe a stack of paper cups.

Not long after settling in, people in the sanctuary could hear sirens. Maggie noticed Mr. Pouliot watching from the corner. It looked as if he was trying to hide behind the tree, like the world's creepiest Christmas surprise. Maggie also noticed a few presents near his feet. *Where did those come from?*

Soon, four police officers and a dog joined them in the sanctuary. This made Maggie miss Eddie.

After chatting with the police, Pastor cleared his throat. He looked incredibly sad. "If I could have your attention guys, it seems that some prescription meds have gone missing. The police are going to do a search of the premises to see if they can locate the meds. Anyone who does not stay in the sanctuary until they are done will be asked to leave the church. This is serious, guys. Please be patient."

Maggie was scared to turn and look at Pouliot, but she did, and he was smiling.

A man Maggie didn't know stood up and said, "Pastor, they need a warrant to go through my stuff."

Pastor replied through tight lips, "You are all guests of this church. I give them permission to go through anything they want to."

The man sat down. Maggie looked around the large room, trying to see if anyone looked guilty.

Everyone looked guilty. And people were oddly quiet. Many were squirming in their seats. And despite how cold it was outside, it seemed to be getting hotter in the sanctuary.

After more than an hour, the police returned. One of them handed Pastor a grocery bag. He looked in it, and then reached in and took out a single bottle of pills. "Dale Prescott," he said, and Dale went down front. Pastor handed him the bottle. "Rita Juarez," he announced, looking at another bottle, and the kitchen tyrant went down front to get her pills. Then she stood next to Dale. Pastor reached back into the bag. "Rita again," he said softly, and handed her another bottle. Then it was, "Jaime Cox," and "Hershel Green." Name after name, Pastor handed out the meds, and people lined up by the altar, until there were less than a dozen people left sitting in the pews.

The police removed Jaime from the lineup, to "ask him a few questions."

"As for the rest of you," Pastor began, "go line up outside the office. One by one, give Cari your meds, and she will put them in the safe for you ..."

"Gonna need a bigger safe," Jackie snorted.

"And from now on, when you need medication, you'll have to go to the office."

"But sometimes the office is locked up," Beau complained.

"Well, you'll have to get there when it's unlocked."

The people up front filed out of the sanctuary and headed toward the office.

Jackie and Maggie headed to their room. Maggie was supposed to have a haircut this morning, but she knew her first appointment was in the meds line, so she lay down. She wanted to discuss what had just happened, but she didn't know what to say, and she knew Jackie wasn't the chatty type. Soon though, Harmony and Gertrude joined them, and Harmony *was* the chatty type. Somehow, she had managed to get the scoop in line, and she filled them in. According to the Open Door grapevine, Jaime had a whole stash of pills in his bag. He was selling and trading them. They had found Clarissa's meds in his stash. He had been arrested and, according to Harmony, was in some serious trouble.

Jackie said, "Can't believe that code guy was here for all that. What are the chances?"

"Oh yeah," Harmony added. "That guy talked to the cops too, and I heard the cops say that our church wasn't breaking any laws. Then the guy was on the phone for a while. I heard him say, 'This is no church,' and I was all like, 'This is more church than any other church.'"

Maggie didn't really know if that made any sense, but she nodded.

A few minutes later, Maggie's appointment showed up at her door. "Are you ready?"

"Yep," Maggie said. She got up, grabbed her supplies, and followed the woman to the bathroom, ready for another day's work. When she got to the bathroom, she discovered that someone had placed a jar on the sink. In black marker, they had written "TIPS" on the jar. This struck Maggie as incredibly funny. And when she finished the haircut, and the woman dropped twenty cents into the jar, Maggie felt incredibly honored.

Chapter 20

Pastor took down the "no men allowed" sign, propped the bathroom door open with a stack of hymnals, and designated Harmony Maggie's official assistant. Harmony took her new duty, which she coined "Magg's bodyguard," seriously. The new rule was that Maggie couldn't be alone in the bathroom with a man. Harmony made sure of it.

Just when Maggie was sure she had trimmed every head in the church, a new person appeared. Her name was Sally, and she looked to be at least 70. Maggie, trying to engage in the usual salon banter, asked Sally when she had gotten to the shelter.

Sally laughed. "Oh, I'm not at the shelter. I just came for a haircut."

Harmony snorted.

"Seriously?" Maggie asked. "How did you know I was giving haircuts?"

"I was at the food cupboard, and there were some girls there talking about you and bragging about their new hairdos."

Maggie couldn't believe it. Who would go to a homeless shelter to get a haircut? But, she did the best she could, and the woman left happy.

The next day, she had another outside customer. Alice had two little girls, one of them with crooked bangs. "I tried to do it myself," she explained. "Can you fix it?"

"I can try," Maggie said, unsure of herself. She got the bangs even, but they became disturbingly short. "You know what would look really cute on you?" Maggie asked the little girl.

The girl just looked up at her, her wide eyes suggesting fear. It occurred to Maggie then, *Why wouldn't this girl be afraid? She's in a folding metal chair in a weird church bathroom.*

"A headband!" Maggie answered herself. "You could use a headband to push your bangs back off your face. Or a scarf, or anything!"

Alice looked panicked. "Hang on," Harmony said, and disappeared. She was back in a few minutes with a plastic headband. "Here, try this," she said. The little girl slid the headband on, and sure enough, the bangs mostly disappeared beneath it. The little girl's face lit up, and Maggie heard Alice sigh in relief.

The girl hopped out of the chair to go admire herself more closely in the mirror, and her sister took her place. Maggie trimmed her sister up, and then offered to do the same for Alice.

"Oh no, you've done enough. Thank you," Alice said, and dropped two crumpled dollar bills in the tip jar.

As they left, a happy little family, Maggie asked Harmony, "Are people really this poor?"

Harmony looked stunned, and then a little irritated. "Where you been?" she asked.

Fresh out of appointments, Maggie and her assistant decided to go to the kitchen for a coffee break. But they didn't get far before they ran into a policeman. "Ladies, could you please head into the sanctuary?"

"Oh now what?" Harmony said with no little attitude. They entered the sanctuary to find many church guests already in there. "What's going on?" Harmony asked Dale.

"Not sure," Dale answered. "They're carrying around a photo, so I'd guess they're looking for someone. It's not me though," Dale laughed. "No one ever looks for me."

Maggie looked at Dale, concerned. *What a bizarre thing to say*, she thought, and then suddenly, she was absolutely sure the police were looking for *her*. This was absurd, of course, but the more she thought about it, the more she became convinced Kirk had sent the police after her. She felt her face flush hot, and she couldn't sit still in her chair.

Squirming around, she noticed a man she hadn't seen before staring at her. He was gorgeous. "Who's that?" she asked, elbowing Harmony.

Harmony looked, "I don't know, but he's hot," she confirmed, accentuating the "t" as if the letter itself were hot.

As one of the police officers strode down the center aisle, Maggie noticed that these were not the same police who had searched for the prescription drugs. It took her another second to realize that these were state police. This caused her panic to worsen. *Kirk has sent the staties after me.*

One of the policemen cleared his throat and announced, "Can someone please point us toward who is in charge?"

No one moved.

The officer waited a second and then added, "Look, no one is in trouble, but we need to speak to who is in charge. Your priest, or reverend, or whatever," he said, without so much as a hint of reverence, "doesn't seem to be on the premises, so we need to speak to whoever is in charge when he's gone."

No one responded. Maggie realized that she didn't know who was in charge. She reasoned no one else did either. The policeman looked frustrated.

"Can I help you?" Cari asked from the back of the room.

The policeman strode toward her. "Are you in charge?" he asked.

"Not exactly," Cari answered. "But I can probably help. What's up?" As the policeman closed the gap between them, their voices became harder to hear, and Maggie strained to listen.

"Who is in charge then, when the priest is away?" the policeman probed.

"God," Cari answered, and Maggie craned her head around, not sure she had heard right.

"God?" the policeman asked, mockingly.

"This is a church, officer, so yes, God is in charge. These people are our guests, not our prisoners. They don't need our supervision."

"And have you seen this man?" the policeman said, shoving a photo in Cari's face. "Cause I guarantee, this guy needs some supervision."

Maggie was relieved that they were officially looking for a man, and annoyed that she couldn't see the photo from where she sat. She also noticed that the attractive man was watching her, not the scene unfolding behind them. This made her feel good.

"I have not seen that man," Cari answered calmly. "Who is he?"

"Well, we've received word that he's hiding out here."

"You're welcome to look, but I haven't seen him."

The policeman stepped back from Cari. He was red-faced and looked as though he was trying to control his temper. "We *are* looking, ma'am. That's why we're here. But we'd also assumed you keep some kind of records here, not just let criminals wander in and out."

The word criminals gave Maggie a start. She took the comment personally, even though she realized the cop was probably looking for one criminal in particular and didn't mean to insult the rest of the law-abiding citizens seated in the sanctuary. She couldn't believe how calm Cari remained.

"I can assure you that the man in the photograph has not spoken to me about staying overnight, but that doesn't mean he's not here. We don't post sentries at the door."

"Perfect," the officer snarled, and turned to walk to the front of the sanctuary.

Maggie sighed, crossed her arms, and tipped her head back. Even staring at the ceiling, she could tell the good-looking guy was still watching her.

After another 20 wasted minutes, two officers joined the cranky one in the front of the sanctuary. They talked for a minute, and then left. A few minutes later, Cari reappeared in the back of the sanctuary. "You can all leave now. False alarm."

Maggie made a beeline for Cari in order to get the scoop, but Mr. Handsome cut her off. "Hi, I'm Levi," he said, stepping into her path. His eyes were icy blue and made it a little hard for her to breathe. Her stomach did a cartwheel.

Harmony stepped between them in an obvious interference maneuver. "Hi," she cooed, "I'm Harmony."

Levi smiled at her, but then returned his gaze to Maggie. "Maggie," she said, and tried to move toward Cari again. Levi's head followed her, but Harmony physically blocked the rest of him from doing so. Free of them both, Maggie tried to find Cari, but she had disappeared. She wasn't in the office either. After several minutes, Maggie found her outside having a cigarette. "What on earth was that?" Maggie asked.

Cari rolled her eyes and exhaled, creating a giant smoke cloud that hovered between them. "I don't know. They said they got some tip that some fugitive was hiding out here. Bet you a million bucks who their tipster was."

"Who?" Maggie asked, clueless.

"Pouliot," Cari spat out.

"The code guy?" Maggie asked.

"Yeah, the code guy. Wish I knew what his problem was."

The two stood there for a minute, silent, and then Maggie said, "So who's the new guy ... Levi?"

Cari looked at her as if she had said something wrong. "Why do you ask?"

"I don't know, just curious," Maggie said, wondering how she had offended Cari. "He's cute is all."

"But you have G," Cari said.

"I don't *have* anyone," Maggie snapped. "Galen and I are just friends."

"If you say so," Cari said, stomping out her cigarette. Then she headed back inside without another word.

Well that was kind of rude, Maggie thought. With nowhere else to go, she headed back to her room. She had just enough time for a nap before Bible study. Relieved to find the room empty, she collapsed onto her top bunk and tried not to think about Levi.

She awoke a few minutes later to Gertrude shaking her.

"What?" she snapped, before she could rein in her tongue.

"G is looking for you," Gertrude said.

"Oh," Maggie sat up abruptly, and rapped her head on the ceiling. "Thanks. Where is he?"

"Kitchen."

"Thanks," Maggie said again. After a quick yawn and stretch, she headed that way.

She found him having coffee with Dale. "Hey," he said, looking up. "I hear you had some excitement around here!"

She nodded and slid into the seat next to him. "Yep, it's important that the cops visit twice weekly, apparently." She noticed Levi sitting alone with his own hot beverage. She tried not to make eye contact.

"Who's that guy?" Galen asked.

"Who?" Maggie said.

Galen nodded toward Levi, "That guy. The one who can't take his eyes off you."

"Oh. That's Levi. He's new I guess."

Galen didn't say anything, so after a few awkward seconds, Maggie snuck a look at him. He looked hurt. "Well, I thought you might want to hang out with Eddie while I was at worship team practice," he said.

"Oh yes, thank you," Maggie said jumping up. Galen gave her his truck keys.

She hung out with Eddie, in Galen's truck, for about a half hour, but then decided to head into church early. She had this nagging feeling that something was bothering Galen, so she wanted to be closer to him.

Galen was up front, fiddling with his guitar. She walked up to him and tried to smile, but he avoided eye contact. She handed him his keys. "Thanks," he said, shoving them in his pocket.

"No, thank *you*. Will you sit with me when you're done playing?" He looked up then, looked her in the eyes, and nodded stoically. "OK, great," she said, and turned to find a seat, even though there was still about 10 minutes before the service would start. She spent those 10 minutes analyzing Galen's behavior. Something was hurting him, and that was hurting her a little.

Chapter 21

Maggie entered the sanctuary the following morning for Sunday service and was stunned to see piles and piles of wrapped presents under the tree. *Where had all those come from?* And she was thrilled to see Galen already seated in a pew, reading his Bible. She hadn't gotten him to talk the night before, so she still didn't know what was wrong.

"Hey, you," she said, sliding into the pew beside him.

"Hey," he said with a smile that suggested everything was back to normal.

"Thought you were a Saturday night guy?" she asked.

"I am," he agreed, "but Gertrude is moving today, so I told her I'd help her. I've got her cats in the truck, ready for their new home."

"Like I said ... angel," Maggie pronounced. "So she actually found an apartment that would take her five cats?"

"I don't know," he said. "I guess so. Want to help ..."

Before Galen could finish his sentence, Levi threw himself into the pew in front of them and turned his icy eyes on Maggie. "Hey," he said provocatively.

"Hi," Maggie said, caught off guard. She felt Galen stiffen beside her.

"Wanna have lunch with me after church?" he asked.

Maggie fought the urge to laugh. *Is he asking me out? To a homeless shelter lunch?* "Um, no thank you. I have plans," Maggie said.

Levi's face went from surprised to offended to cocky in less than a second. "Fine, I see how it is," he said coolly, and stalked off.

"Well, that was bizarre," she said. Galen just looked at her. "So yes," she announced, "there is nothing I would like better than to help Gertrude move."

Galen smirked, but he didn't look exactly happy.

Pastor preached about attacks from the enemy, and Maggie inferred he was talking, at least in part, about the code enforcer and the police. "We don't need to be afraid," he said, softly but confidently. "God knows what's going to happen before it happens, and he already knows how he will fix it. We will be OK. God is not going to let us starve or freeze. He promises to provide for us if we put our trust in him. Right?"

There were a few "amens" and "hallelujahs," but for the most part, the Sunday morning crowd was pretty tame. Had he asked that question at a Friday night Bible study, someone might have even argued with him.

Pastor gave an altar call, and Maggie noticed for the first time that Sally, her hair "client" was in church. Maggie might not have noticed at all, but Sally was on her way to the altar. She knelt, and it looked as if it hurt her knees. Maggie was suddenly overcome with a desire to pray for her. In a rare lack of self-consciousness, Maggie went to her knees right there in front of her pew and began to pray fervently. She stayed that way until she heard the worship team fire it up. Pulling herself to her feet, she looked around for Sally, and found her in the front row. *Unbelievable*, Maggie thought, *did God actually use my bathroom-salon to bring someone to Christ?* Maggie, truly overwhelmed, wiped her tears on her shirt and then lifted both arms into the air, unabashedly. Sally might have been the one who had just found Jesus, but Maggie felt as though she was the one having the breakthrough.

After the closing prayer, Maggie grabbed Galen's arm. "Can you give me a minute before you leave?"

"Of course," Galen said, and Maggie noticed he was looking at her with tenderness.

Maggie weaved through the crowd until she found Sally. Sally's face lit up when she saw her. "Can I give you a hug?" Maggie asked.

"Of course," Sally said, her voice still shaky with tears.

"It's so good to see you here!" Maggie said into her ear.

"What's that, honey?" Sally asked.

Maggie laughed. And again, over the din, said more loudly, "I'm glad to see you here!"

"Well good," Sally said with a laugh, "'cause I think you'll be seeing me more often!"

"Great," Maggie said, and gently squeezed her thin arm again. Then she turned to find Galen. He was standing by the door, watching her. She made her way to him. "Thank you," she said.

"No problem. Gertrude wants to eat first anyway. Then we'll load her up." He smiled.

"OK cool, let's go eat," she said.

They headed downstairs and got in line. Gertrude got up from her tray and headed over to them. "The cats are cold," she said to Galen accusingly.

"They're fine," Galen said. "Go finish your lunch and then we'll take them to your new place and get them warmed right   up."

"Why can't they be inside your truck? Why do they have to be in the back, where it's cold?"

Galen seemed to have mastered the handling of Gertrude. "Go eat," he said gently, but emphatically. "All this is almost over."

"Wow," Maggie said, "you always know what to say."

"You're kidding, right?" Galen said.

"What's that supposed to mean?" Maggie asked, but they had reached the front of the line and Galen handed her a tray instead of answering her.

They found a spot at the far end of the room, where the heat didn't quite reach. "So did you see all those presents?" Maggie asked.

"You mean under the tree?"

"Yeah."

"Yep, happens every year. I'm never really sure where they come from, but people from the community step up. Some are from other churches. Some from local businesses."

"Other churches?" Maggie asked. "I'm surprised. I've kind of gotten the impression that other churches don't like us."

"I don't think it's that," Galen said thoughtfully. "I think they like what we're doing. It's just that, sometimes, when someone does something differently, you take it as a criticism that you're not doing things right. Do you know what I mean?"

"Not really," Maggie said, feeling a little slow.

"Oh, maybe it's my imagination, I don't know. The other churches will give us money and donate items. But sometimes they act like what we're doing here is a criticism against them, like they should be doing it too."

"Well, they should be, shouldn't they?" Maggie asked.

"I honestly don't know … I mean, people make up different parts of the Body, right? Like we all have special functions to perform. Maybe it's like that with churches. Maybe some churches are supposed to be homeless shelters, some are supposed to focus on children's ministry, and some … I don't know … maybe some specialize in knitting hats for the homeless shelter church? You know what I mean?"

"I think I do," Maggie mused. "And I also think that my job as a Body member is to cut hair. I gotta say, I never saw that coming. Never really thought hair was going to turn into a ministry."

"Yep," Galen agreed, "and I never thought I'd be operating an animal shelter out of my garage. But here we are."

They finished eating, and then headed back to Maggie's room. She felt strangely proud to bring Galen to her room. She'd spent so much time at his place, it was kind of fun to welcome him into hers. But when they got into the room, she felt less proud. It looked like they were having a garage sale.

"What's all this?" Maggie asked, even though there was no one there to answer her except Galen.

"I don't know," he said.

Gertrude appeared just then, making Maggie wonder how a plump woman with a walker could be so stealthy. "Are you here to help me with my stuff?" Gertrude asked.

"Yes," Galen answered.

"Great! Careful with this one," she said, kicking a trash bag with her foot. "It's very heavy."

Galen picked it up and then looked at her suspiciously. "That it is. What is in this exactly?"

"Just my stuff. Maggie, you can probably lift that one." She pointed at another bag with her chin.

"Gertrude," Maggie started, "you didn't have this much stuff yesterday. What is all this?"

"Just my stuff," Gertrude snapped. "I said it's my stuff, and it's my stuff."

Galen set the bag back down. "I think what Maggie is trying to say is, we are worried that you might have accidentally taken some things that belong to the church, or to other people here."

Gertrude's eyes grew wide. "A thief? You're calling me a thief? I'm not a thief!"

"OK, so you won't mind if I take a peek?"

"Of course I mind! Stay out of my stuff!"

But Galen ignored her and opened the trash bag. "Um, Gertrude, this looks like actual garbage. Where did you get this stuff?"

"It's not garbage. Just because someone throws something away, doesn't make it garbage."

"Ah," Galen said as if he understood.

Maggie didn't understand any of it. She bent down and opened a box at her feet. It was full of Bibles. "What are these Gertrude?"

"Those are Bibles."

Maggie couldn't help it. She was exasperated. "I know they're Bibles. Why are you taking them?"

"The sign in the office said 'free Bibles.'"

"Well, it meant one free Bible for one person, so why don't you pick one?"

"You know what?" Gertrude practically shrieked. "Maybe I don't need your help after all. I'll just do it myself." She certainly looked determined, but she didn't move a muscle.

"No, you don't have to do that," Galen said gently. "We'll help you." He hefted the garbage bag over one shoulder and picked up another one with his other hand. Then he headed out the door.

Maggie grabbed one of the Bibles from the box and looked around for something else to lug. "Where'd you get the crockpot?"

"I actually have two. Someone donated them. Cari said I could have them."

"OK," Maggie sighed and put the Bible in a crockpot. Then she found the other one, and, with one crockpot under each arm, she headed for the parking lot.

"Are you sure about this?" she asked Galen when she got there.

"About what?"

"About helping her move all this stuff. Look at this! She has two crockpots!"

"If I see anything that looks stolen, I'll speak up, but I think mostly this is just junk."

"OK," she said, and loaded the crockpots into the back of the truck.

Eventually, they were loaded up. Maggie climbed into the middle of the cab, and Eddie scrambled onto her lap. She had left the door open for Gertrude, but now Gertrude just stood there staring into the empty cab. "You can get in," Maggie said.

"I can't."

Galen had started toward the driver's side, but now he turned around and headed back toward Gertrude. "How can I help?" he asked.

Gertrude looked at him helplessly. Maggie didn't think she had a plan. "OK, put your arm around my shoulder here," Galen said, squatting down so she could reach his shoulder more easily. "And can you get your left foot right here?" he asked, nodding toward the running board. She nodded and grunted as she hoisted her foot. "OK, now you push with that foot as I lift. Ready? One, two, three!" And then they both grunted as Galen lifted Gertrude into his pickup.

When Galen finally got himself into the truck, Maggie couldn't help but stare at him.

"What?" he asked.

Maggie just shook her head, speechless.

Gertrude's new home was in a trailer park. Gertrude told Galen the address and he quickly found the empty trailer. She fumbled with the lock for a while, until Galen took the key away from her and unlocked the door. Then he began to unload.

"Aren't you coming in?" Gertrude hollered to Maggie. Grudgingly, Maggie grabbed a few trash bags herself.

"I'm assuming you don't need five dog crates, so you just want me to bring the cats in?" Galen asked after several trips.

"Sure, but be careful, 'cause sometimes Thunder bites."

"Which one's Thunder?"

"I don't know."

Galen paused. "You don't know which cat is which?"

"No, of course *I* know," Gertrude answered, as if he was stupid. "But I don't know how to explain it to *you*. It's just Thunder. I know him when I see him."

"OK." Galen gave up and went outside. He came back in with a cat in each hand.

"Neither of those is Thunder," Gertrude said, answering a question no one had asked.

Galen went back out for another trip, and Maggie followed. He handed her a dark gray cat who did look like he could have a mean streak. Maggie held him out in front of her as she walked back into the trailer. As soon as she was inside, the cat screamed and leapt out of her hands, flying through midair until it landed, on all fours of course, in the middle of the living room.

"Thunder!" Gertrude cried and sort of walker-galloped down the trailer to him. She scooped him up and covered him in kisses. "Oh, Thunder, you've got to be more careful!"

Galen was back then with two less dramatic cats, which he gently set down on the floor. "OK, Gertrude, you going to be OK here?" he asked, looking around.

"Yep," she said, still kissing Thunder.

"Are you sure? You don't have any furniture."

"Oh, I'll get some, don't you worry," she said. "Stuff has a way of just finding me."

"OK," he said, feeling in his coat pockets for something that wasn't there. "Hang on, I'll be right back." He was back within seconds with a scrap of paper and a pen. "Here," he said, writing on the paper, "this is my phone number. Call me if you need anything or get into trouble, OK?"

Gertrude didn't even look at him. She just nodded.

"OK then, we're going to go," Galen said. He waited briefly for some response from Gertrude, but didn't act surprised when he didn't get one. "OK, let's go," he said more quietly to Maggie. They headed out and hopped into the truck.

She was staring at him again. She knew it, and she couldn't seem to stop herself.

"What?" he asked again.

"Sorry, you're just so … I'm just … you're …" he started the truck. "I've just never known anyone like you. I mean, we're all supposed to love others, right? But you, you like really *do it*." She paused. "You're just amazing, that's all."

He put the truck in reverse and started to back out of Gertrude's drive, but he didn't look as if he'd received the compliment very well.

"I'm sorry, did I say something wrong?" Maggie asked.

"No, you didn't. I'm just … if I'm so amazing, then why are you gaga for that Levi guy?"

Whoa. It practically knocked the wind out of her. She tried to catch her breath, frantically scanning her brain for a way to fix this. "Galen, I'm not gaga over Levi. I promise … And you are amazing."

He glanced at her as he put the truck in drive. "I'm sorry. I didn't mean to unload on you. I just … you seem to enjoy spending time with me. You call me amazing, tell me I'm an angel, yet none of this is good enough for you?" The last few words flew out of his mouth, as if he were forcing them out.

"What? What are you talking about?"

"Maggie, obviously, I like you. And it's OK if you don't like me back. I can live with that. But it's just hard living with you acting like you like me and talking like you like me, but not liking me. I mean," he looked at her again, "what's wrong with me? If I'm so amazing, what's wrong with me?"

Maggie's throat filled with a painful lump, and she began to study her hands. After a few seconds, she said, "I'm sorry, Galen. I didn't mean for it to be like this. And I didn't know you liked me. And I do like you. You are more than good enough for me, Galen, I've meant everything I've said. It's just …"

"It's just what?" he asked, and she could hear weariness in his voice.

"Oh, Galen, I just can't. I'm sorry." She was crying now, giant tears wetting her scarf.

"Why?"

"Why?" she repeated. "I don't know, I just can't."

He pulled the truck into an empty parking lot. He put it in park and then turned to look at her. "Why?" he repeated.

She took a deep breath. "I don't how to explain it. I'm just ..." She rolled her eyes. "Look, can we not do this right now?"

"Sure, we don't have to do this right now. But you just told me you like me. So then ..."

She was still staring at her hands, concentrating on listening for what he would say next, so she didn't notice at first that he was sliding across the seat toward her. Then he took her chin in his hand, and gently turned her face toward his. He just looked into her eyes. She had plenty of time to pull away, to make an excuse, to say no. Part of her brain was screaming at her to escape. But she didn't. And he leaned toward her and kissed her gently. His lips lingered for a few seconds, but there wasn't much movement. He didn't try to pry her lips open or tickle her tongue, and for that she was grateful. When he pulled away, she was sad that he did.

"There. Was that so bad?" he said, smiling, looking a little proud of himself.

"No, of course not. Galen, I do like you. It's just, it's complicated. You don't understand. I was in a horrible relationship. And I'm not OK. We could start something here, we could get involved, but I know that I would end up disappointing you. I just can't do this."

"OK," Galen said, putting the truck back in drive. He was no longer smiling, and no longer looking proud. He looked sad.

Chapter 22

The night that Galen kissed her, Maggie couldn't fall asleep. She couldn't stop thinking about the kiss. It had been so *different*. Not that she had a lot of experience in the kissing department. She'd made out with a few boys when she was in high school, but she had gotten together with Kirk so young that he was all she really remembered. And it seemed as though, with them, especially Kirk, kissing was a means to an end. Kirk had kissed her so that he could get to something else.

When Galen kissed her, it felt as though he was kissing her just for the sake of kissing her. He didn't seem to have an agenda. Finally, she did fall asleep, and she slept deeply until she woke to someone licking her nose. She opened her eyes to see Eddie. Relieved it wasn't Dale, she rubbed her eyes and looked around the room, which was flooded with sunshine. Galen was leaning on the other set of bunk beds. "I smuggled him in for a quick visit," Galen said. "Don't tell."

She laughed. "Why?"

"Well, I needed his help to apologize."

She was suddenly very self-conscious. Oh great, they're going to do this here? Now? She hadn't even brushed her teeth yet. She vowed to start sleeping in a bra. "You don't need to apologize, Galen."

"Yes I do. I shouldn't have pushed."

"No really, Galen, it's OK." She paused and swung her legs over the edge of the bed, only half sitting up so she didn't rap her head again. "It was an amazing kiss. It's just that," she wanted to get this out, but she found she couldn't look at him, so she threw herself back down on the bed and stared up at the stained ceiling. "It's just that kissing and romance and all of it leads to an intimacy that I just can't handle."

She waited for Galen to say something. He didn't.

"Does that make sense?" she said, finally looking at him.

"Not really, but I'm a guy, so I'm probably missing something." He uncrossed his arms and shoved his hands in his pockets. "You live in a teensy room with three other women. You have no privacy, no secrets, and you are perfectly comfortable picking bugs out of other people's hair. It sounds to me like you're OK with intimacy."

She saw then where her communication had failed her, and very quietly, she said, "I meant *physical* intimacy."

He crossed the room then, quickly, and took one of her hands in his. With the other hand, he smoothed back the curls from her forehead. "Maggie, this is not a race. I would *never* do anything to make you feel uncomfortable. I'm sorry that Kirk is a jerk. I'm sorry you had to go through that. But I'm not him. I would never do anything but honor you and love you."

She felt a tear slide out of the corner of the eye closest to Galen. *Good grief,* she thought. *He's going to think I'm a mental mushroom. It is too early in the morning for tears.* Eddie, sensing something was wrong, pawed at her chin. She turned her face toward Galen, "So we go through all this. We get close, and then we find out that I'm broken? Aren't you going to regret all your effort and time?"

He kissed her on the forehead and said, "No. First of all, you're not broken. Second of all, I would never regret time spent with you, no matter what happens. Let's just give it a try?"

She sighed shakily and returned her gaze to the ceiling. "OK," she said, but it came out more like a reluctant acquiescence than a ringing endorsement. "Can I just think about it for a while?"

"Sure. If I can ask you a personal question?"

"Sure," she said, figuring the conversation couldn't get much more personal.

"Have you ever been physically intimate with a husband who loves God and loves you?"

Well, she was wrong. "Obviously not," she said.

"OK then. I promise you. When that happens, it will be different. It will be safe. It will be a good thing. It won't be scary. Whether it's me or another God-fearing man, it's something you can look forward to." He took a step back then, and that was a good thing, because she needed some time to absorb the weight of his words. He grabbed Eddie with one hand, gave her hand one last squeeze with the other, and said, "See you later." And he was gone.

And she already missed him.

She got up, and realized she had slept through breakfast again. She showered, dressed, turned down two haircut requests, and found her way to the sanctuary. She plopped down on the front pew and stared at the cross hanging in front of her.

"What's up?" Cari asked from behind, startling her.

"Oh nothing."

"Don't lie to me," she said, sitting down beside her. She patted Maggie's leg. "Come on, tell Cari all about it."

"Where did all the presents come from?" Maggie tried to redirect her. They were now mounded up so high they hid the bottom of the tree.

"Oh, here, there, everywhere. Now don't try to change the subject."

"I saw name tags though. So those presents are for specific people?"

Cari sighed. "No, when I get donations, I figure out who could use them, who would like them, and I wrap them up and label them accordingly."

Maggie smiled. "Does that mean I'm getting a hairdryer?"

Cari laughed. "No, nobody has donated a hairdryer yet. Sorry. If one comes in though, it's yours. Now stop beating around the bush. What's got you in a tizzy? G do something wrong?"

"No, he never does anything wrong," Maggie sighed. "It's me. I don't know, I mean, he's perfect, but I'm just not really that physically attracted to him. And I don't even know if it's his fault. Maybe it's just that I'm not attracted to any man. Maybe I'm just too damaged."

"Did he hit you?"

"What? Galen? No! Galen would never hit me!"

"Not G, silly, the last guy."

"Oh," Maggie said softly. "Yeah, not a lot. Mostly he was just rough."

"Yeah, I know the type," Cari said convincingly. "I used to get the crap beat out of me more often than not. If my husband drank, he got mean. And he drank a lot. And you know what? All those bruises didn't hurt as much as the idea that I deserved them. Stupid jerk actually managed to convince me that *he* was putting up with *me*. Sicko. Anyway, I hear ya, but you know G's not like that, right?"

"Of course I do. But does God really want me to get involved with a man I'm not really attracted to?"

"I don't know, have you asked him?"

"Asked him what?" Maggie asked, confused.

"Have you asked God if Galen is the man for you?"

"Well, no," Maggie said, wondering why she hadn't thought of that.

"OK, well, I'll leave you to it. Here's how I pray in these situations: 'God, I'm really dumb. Please make your will painfully obvious to me.'"

Maggie laughed, but Cari was already walking away, off to solve some other crisis. So Maggie prayed, "God, thank you for bringing me here. I know that you know what you're doing. But I'm confused right now, God. I thought you wanted me to be single. Is that not what you want? I like Galen, of course. He's the kindest, sweetest man I've ever met, and I know he loves you. But I don't get that warm, fuzzy feeling with him. I don't get butterflies in my stomach like I used to get in the beginning with Kirk. Does that even matter, God? Is that what you're trying to tell me? That I have to trade the butterflies for a practical choice? I don't know, God. Look, I'm really dumb. And I need you to please make your will painfully obvious to me. I do want to please you God, I do. I also want to be happy. And I really, really don't want to hurt Galen. Amen."

She got up, marveling at how quiet the sanctuary was when no one was in it.

Chapter 23

Later that afternoon, Mr. Pouliot brought the actual *Mayor* to the shelter. Maggie was giving Dale a much-needed trim, and she saw Mr. Pouliot and another suit walk by the open door. Maggie frowned at Harmony, who said, "I'll go find out," leaving Maggie and Dale alone in the bathroom, which was totally against salon policy. She was back soon, however, to report that Mr. Pouliot couldn't get the police to do anything, so he had brought the Mayor.

"Good grief," Maggie said, "doesn't the Mayor have better things to do?"

"Just how busy do you think the Mattawooptock Mayor is, Maggie?" Dale asked.

"Good point," Maggie said.

"Tomorrow's Christmas Eve," Dale said.

"Yep," Maggie said.

"So what did you get G?" he asked.

Oh no. "Like I'm gonna tell you," Maggie said, trying to cover up the truth. *What am I going to get him? I have no money!*

"Are you done?" Dale asked.

Maggie realized she had stopped cutting. "Oh yeah, go ahead and look in the mirror and see what you think."

"Don't need to. I trust you completely. See you ladies later," and Dale was gone.

"You didn't get him anything, did you?" Harmony accused.

"No, I didn't even think of it! I'm destitute, and homeless! What can I get him?"

"What have you been doing with your tips?" she asked.

Maggie laughed. "I've put all six dollars of them in the offering plate."

"Well, that was silly!" Harmony laughed.

Suddenly, Maggie had an idea. "Do you know where we could get some sewing supplies?"

"What do I look like, Mary Stewart?"

"You mean Martha Stewart?" Maggie asked.

"Whatever," Harmony said. "Ask Cari."

Maggie took off to find her. She had no trouble doing so. Cari, Pastor, Mr. Pouliot, and the Mattawooptock Mayor were all crowded into the office. As Maggie came around the corner, she heard a voice she didn't recognize say, "Look, as far as I can tell, there's nothing going on here to be alarmed about. Sure, it's a weird situation, but it's a free country, and if these people want to live in a church, then they get to live in a church." By the time he had finished, Maggie was standing in the doorway.

"Sorry, didn't mean to interrupt. I'll come back later," she said, but she didn't go far. She stood next to the door, just out of view, straining to hear.

She heard Mr. Pouliot say, "You, as Mayor, have a chance to shut this whole thing down. This shelter is giving our town a reputation. It's putting a strain on our hospital. Our crime rates are going up. These people are spending their days walking up and down *our* streets, scaring off potential businesses—"

The Mayor interrupted, "Lance, you're getting a little carried away. Our crime rate hasn't gone up. Don't be ridiculous."

"Well, it will! Mark my words! It's even attracting out-of-staters. People from Massachusetts are coming all the way to Mattawooptock just to live for free!" Maggie's stomach rolled.

"OK, well, Lance, you've made your point. I've listened. I've taken the tour. I think these people are just trying to do good. Everyone seems safe. I think you have a problem, Lance, and it's not this church. Good day, folks."

Maggie scurried down the hall before anyone could see her. She made a lap around the entire complex, wandering aimlessly; then she headed back for Cari. She found her and Pastor Dan in the office.

"What do you need, Maggie?" Cari asked, looking up.

"Is everything OK?" Maggie asked.

Pastor answered, "Yes, absolutely. The Mayor is a good man."

"OK, good, well, I was just wondering Cari, if you had like a mini sewing kit I could borrow? Maybe some scraps of cloth too?"

Cari raised an eyebrow. "Doing some late Christmas shopping?" she asked.

"Sort of," Maggie said.

Cari unlocked a door in the back of the office. "Come on in," she said. The closet was packed floor to ceiling with office supplies, toiletries, and weird odds and ends.

It's a good thing Gertrude never found this stash, Maggie thought. Cari moved a pair of tiny swim trunks, a bag of plastic butter knives, and what looked like an actual lobster buoy out of the way and came to a pile of rags.

"Will any of this work?" Maggie took a step closer and saw some perfect off-white cotton. She grabbed it. Cari opened another plastic container that was full of thread and needles. Maggie grabbed some black thread and a giant needle. "I think that's a yarn needle," Cari warned.

"That's OK," Maggie said. She had no idea what she was doing, but didn't want to admit it.

"Anything else?" Cari asked.

"Do you have any stuffing?"

Cari chuckled. "What on earth are you up to?" she said, digging through what looked like Sunday school prizes from 1970. This led to a pile of Open Door Church Softball Team hats, which were several clashing shades of orange.

"Do we still have a softball team?" Maggie asked.

"We sure do, in the spring. You just wait. I've never laughed so hard in my ... you know what? This is foolish. How much stuffing do you need?"

"About the size of a softball."

"Well then, just cut a little hole in the corner of your pillow and use some of that."

"Seriously?"

"Well sure, why not. Then just sew the pillow back up. I won't call the pillow police."

Maggie laughed. "OK," and then she caught sight of a small ball of brown yarn. *Perfect.* "Can I have that too?"

Cari handed it to her. "Good grief, what are you making G, a *doll*?"

Chapter 24

Maggie's bathroom was strangely quiet on the day before Christmas. Apparently, no one was in the mood for a haircut. She waited as long as she could stand it, and then, at about 11, called Galen.

"Hey I totally understand if you're busy with the holidays and all, but I would love to see you today?" She was actually nervous. *Why am I nervous?*

"Yeah of course. I'll be right over."

She didn't even let him get out of the truck. When she saw him pull in, she ran out to meet him. She climbed into the truck, proudly holding her wrapped present in her hand.

"What is that?" he asked teasingly.

She looked up at him to smile, and that's when it happened. The butterflies. And not just a couple either. It was like an *army* of butterflies commandeered her stomach.

"You OK?" he asked, his smile fading.

"Yeah," she said, forcing herself to breathe. She stared straight ahead and tried not to think about what was happening. She couldn't remember being so nervous — ever.

They were at the garage in no time. "I've got a little bit of work to do, but you can head up and hang out with Eddie if you want."

"OK, sure," she said, and then thought better of it. "Is there anything I can help you with?"

Galen laughed, "What, like on cars?"

"Well, I don't know what I'm doing, but maybe you could teach me?"

"Thanks. I'm touched, really, but you go ahead. I don't want Eddie to get mad at me for hogging you, and I won't be long. Just got to finish up a few things."

She couldn't help but feel a little rejected, but she headed up the stairs. She collapsed on the couch and flipped through the many channels until she landed on *Reba*.

After only an episode and a half, Galen was upstairs. "I'm just gonna take a quick shower and then we'll get some lunch. Sound good?"

She smiled up at him. There he stood, in ripped, faded coveralls, covered in oil. He still had bed hair and he needed a shave. And he was easily the most gorgeous thing she had ever seen. She noticed for the first time that his eyes looked like dark chocolate. He took her breath away. "Sure," she said, and just barely managed it.

She tried to focus on *Reba*, but the plot was suddenly too complicated. Galen soon returned and sat beside her on the couch. "You hungry?" he asked.

"Yep."

"What do you feel like?"

Like these butterflies are trying to kill me. "Oh, whatever you want."

He just stared at her.

"OK, Thai."

He smiled and pulled out his phone.

When he was done ordering, Maggie asked, "Can I give you your present now?"

"Don't you want to wait until Christmas?"

"Nah."

"OK, then," he said smiling. Maggie handed him the present. He unwrapped it quickly and Maggie was so excited, anticipating his laughter. He didn't laugh though. He looked at the doll, looked at Maggie, and looked at the doll again.

"It's an Amish doll," she said, thinking he must not have gotten the joke. "She has no face!"

He smiled then, but it definitely wasn't the reaction she was expecting or looking for. "Yeah, I get it," he said.

"I'm sorry, Galen. I didn't have much to work with, so I was trying to be funny. It's easier to do funny on no money than it is thoughtful."

"Really," he smiled. "It's OK. It's still thoughtful; it means you listen to me when I talk. That's a good thing." He took her hand and pulled her off the couch. "And I can honestly say, that is the creepiest Christmas gift I've ever received. I will cherish it always." She laughed then. "Come on, I'll show you what I got you. It's in the garage." She let him lead her down to the garage, and up to a cute little two-door Chevy Spark. He smiled at her.

"What?" she asked.

He opened the driver's side door and motioned as if to invite her to sit in it.

"Galen, I don't understand," she said.

"It's yours, Maggie. I got it for a great price and fixed it up, and now it's yours."

She didn't even say thank you. She just threw her arms around his neck. The hug felt a little awkward until he wrapped his arms around her waist. Then it just felt perfect.

She was thinking about planting her lips on his when he said, "We should go get the Thai food. Want to take your new car?"

"Of course! I'll go get Eddie," she said, already running up the stairs.

It felt so good to drive again. She hadn't realized how much she had missed it. The new car was absolutely awesome. "I can't believe you bought me a car," she said, giggling.

"And I want to be clear, it's a no-strings-attached gift," Galen said. "I don't want you to think that you owe me anything. I just wanted to help."

She smiled at him again. Suddenly, her whole life felt like one big smile.

Chapter 25

Maggie spent Christmas day lying around the shelter being lazy. Galen was with his extended family, and she didn't want to monopolize his time. Well, actually she kind of did, but she didn't want to annoy him.

That morning had been crazy. The men had taken turns guarding the sanctuary doors. No one was allowed near the tree till after breakfast. But once breakfast was over, there was a mad rush. The kids poured up the stairs and while the adults pretended to be nonchalant, most of them were pretty excited too.

No one went without. Every kid had a toy to unwrap and a pair of mittens. Then the kids spent several minutes trading mittens to get the colors they wanted. Some of the adults received blankets. Some got chocolates and peach blossoms. Maggie unwrapped a hairbrush. Everyone was incredibly cordial and calm. Maggie missed Galen.

After presents, people lingered in the sanctuary. There was an abundance of candy canes, and Cari kept carrying trays of hot cocoa up from the kitchen. Maggie stirred hers with a candy cane, creating a delicious combination. Jenny started to play Christmas carols on the piano, and every once in a while, someone would sing along for a few bars.

Soon it was time for Christmas lunch, and what a spread it was! Turkey and ham and more side dishes than they could possibly eat. "Why is there so much food?" Maggie whispered to Harmony.

"I don't know. This is my first Christmas here too, but I'm guessing we'll be eating leftovers for days."

"Fine by me," Maggie said, as a server dropped a yummy-looking spoonful of green bean casserole on her plate. They ate until they couldn't eat any more, and then dragged themselves upstairs. Harmony grabbed a candy cane on the way and stuck the end in her mouth.

"How can you have room for any more?" Maggie asked, laughing.

"I don't," Harmony mumbled without taking the candy out of her mouth, "but doesn't peppermint help with digestion?"

"Oh, OK, well, in that case," Maggie turned around and trotted back to the bowl of candy canes to grab herself one. Then the two girls walked to their room with red and white hooks sticking out of their mouths.

On the way by Maggie's bathroom, Harmony took the candy out of her mouth and held it up. "This looks kind of like a barber pole. We should hang one up outside your door!"

This struck Maggie as unreasonably funny, and she laughed all the way to her room. Jackie was already in there and rolled her eyes when she saw how jovial her roommates were. Maggie and Harmony decided the only reasonable thing to do on Christmas afternoon was to take a nap. As Maggie drifted off to sleep, she realized how much she liked living with Harmony, and how sad she would be if she had to live without her.

Chapter 26

Maggie woke up the next morning unsure of whom she missed more: Galen or Eddie. She did a few haircuts and a dye for a woman who'd heard about Maggie on Facebook, but by afternoon, Maggie couldn't stand it anymore. She drove to Galen's place.

He was working, of course. "Hi!" he said, seeming happy to see her.

"Hey. Wanna hang out? I'm trying to avoid my bathroom."

He laughed at that, and wiped his hands on a rag. "Sure, I was just finishing up on this girl, and then I'll be right up. Go ahead up."

After a quick shower, Galen joined her on the couch. She was watching *Reba* again.

"Don't you ever get sick of this show?" Galen asked.

"Nope. It's hilarious. Plus, Reba always has great hair."

Galen gave in and watched it with her, even laughing once at Van. During a commercial, Galen said, "You make sure you're warm enough tonight."

Well that was a fairly weird thing to say. "OK, why?"

"Didn't you hear the weather report?"

"Nope. The paper boy forgot to drop off my paper this morning."

Galen rolled his eyes. "Well, temperatures are supposed to get down to negative 20, with a wind chill of up to 50 below."

"Oh wow, that's kind of scary."

"Yeah, more than kind of. Expect some extra folks at the church tonight."

Galen was right. Bible study that night was *packed*. Several faces Maggie didn't recognize, many of them children.

The wind was howling. It sounded as if it was trying to rip the roof off. Pastor gave a short message and then encouraged everyone to stay inside. "Save your smoke breaks for morning," he said.

The girls got a new roommate that night. Amy moved in without saying much. She was a gorgeous Asian woman. At least, Maggie thought she was a woman. She could have been as young as 16. Maggie fought the urge to ask.

Maggie had trouble falling asleep that night, but she was plenty warm enough. And for that, she was thankful. It was almost as if she didn't *want* to fall asleep; she just wanted to lie there and enjoy the warmth. She thanked God over and over that both she and Eddie were safe for the night.

Eventually, Maggie did fall asleep, but was awoken less than an hour later by people hollering. She rolled over and Harmony was there, just about to shake her. "What?"

"Fire!" Harmony said. "Gotta go!"

Maggie leapt off the top bunk as Harmony flew out the door. Maggie didn't smell any smoke, but she could hear lots of panicky voices and sirens in the distance. She briefly wondered if this was all a sick prank.

As they stepped outside, the air hit her lungs like a knife. Fire trucks were rolling into the parking lot, sirens blaring. A few cop cars were behind them, and an ambulance brought up the rear.

Oh my gosh, it's real, Maggie thought, as she saw the flames leaping out of the addition's roof. *There were kids in there.* She felt sick to her stomach, but was a little encouraged when she looked around the parking lot. Many, many people had spilled out of the shelter, which Maggie took to mean there couldn't be many left inside. A firefighter asked them to step back, and when they did, Maggie was relieved to see Jackie.

Unfortunately though, people were in their pajamas. A few were wrapped in blankets, but most weren't. Some, including herself, were wearing socks. She didn't notice anyone barefoot, but that didn't mean it wasn't happening. People were huddling up and sharing blankets when Pastor suddenly yelled, "Everybody, get into the parsonage! Get warm!" They didn't have to be told twice. The guests flooded into the parsonage, and Maggie wondered how they would all fit. She followed the crowd and found a spot to sit on the hallway floor. The house was, as she had predicted, packed, and she was grateful to have a wall to lean on. People lined up at the windows to watch the action outside, but Maggie didn't want to look.

"Hey, guys, let's pray," Maggie said, before she even realized what she was saying. Everybody in her immediate vicinity bowed their heads. Too desperate to be nervous, Maggie prayed, "Please, Father, do not let anyone be hurt. Please make sure everyone gets out. Please help and protect the firemen. Please, Father," she pleaded, crying now, "save our home."

What seemed like a long time later, some non-resident church members arrived with pillows and blankets. People took them, some covered up with them, but nobody seemed in the mood for sleeping. There wasn't enough room anyway. Maggie continued to pray silently, until she heard her name. She looked up to see Galen standing over her. Without thinking, she jumped up and fell into him, burying her face in his chest and wrapping her arms around his waist. She wept into his Carhartt. He put his arms around her and rested his chin on her head.

"Come on, let's get out of here," he said.

She didn't want to let go of him.

"Come on, it's OK, everyone is OK," he said, gently pushing her off him. He grabbed her hand and led her out of the parsonage, stepping over several pairs of legs on the way.

The cold air stole her breath again. She saw that the flames were gone, replaced with mass quantities of water and smoke.

She didn't even realize he was guiding her to his truck until he opened the door for her and she saw Eddie. She let go of Galen then and climbed into the truck. Eddie climbed onto her lap and began to lick at her tears. Galen climbed into the driver's seat. It was incredibly warm in the cab, and Maggie caught her breath.

"How did you know?" she managed.

"My cousin is a volunteer firefighter."

Maggie leaned back, watching the firefighters. "It looks like they saved most of the church. Only the addition burned?"

Galen nodded. "But they're not letting anybody back in tonight. Going to wait till morning, make sure it's safe."

"And you're sure everyone is OK?"

"That's what Cari said. Everyone is accounted for, except for one new guy, but the firefighters searched the building and couldn't find him. They figured he took off."

"Took off? Where's he gonna go in this cold?"

Galen sighed. "They think he might have set the fire."

Maggie looked at him wide-eyed. "Someone *set* the fire? Who would do that? Who would burn down a homeless shelter? And why would they choose the coldest night of the year?"

Galen shook his head. "I don't know. You want me to take you to a motel? So you can get some sleep? My treat, of course."

"No, thank you. That's really sweet and generous of you, but I kind of want to stay with everybody else."

"I get it. That makes sense."

Still, they sat in the truck for a long time, watching the firefighters work.

Chapter 27

Early the next morning, the Fire Chief let people back into the church. In the sanctuary or Maggie's room, the only evidence was a faint smell of smoke. But in the addition, where half the guests were living, the damage was catastrophic. The addition had all but disappeared, and the adjacent walls were waterlogged and covered in ice. Volunteers, some from the shelter and some Maggie had never seen before, were hammering up a makeshift wall that entirely cut off that part of the building.

Maggie's bathroom was close enough to the addition that it got sealed off too. For her, this was beyond devastating. Even though her brain knew that she could cut hair anywhere, her heart was broken. That had been her bathroom. That was where she had been reborn. That bathroom, as crazy as it sounded, was who she *was* now. It had given her purpose. It had made her worth something. And it was gone.

Everybody gathered in the kitchen for breakfast, and they were a somber lot. People went through the line mumbling thank you, chose their seats without arguing, and chewed in silence. Most people were finishing up or already dumping their trays when Pastor appeared on the stairs. "Can I have your attention please," he called out from the front of the room.

"Wow," he joked, "that's the quickest you guys have ever gotten quiet." No one laughed. He cleared his throat. "So, I am a tired man this morning, but I am not sad. This is just a building. We don't need to mourn the loss of wood and nails. We can, however, thank our Father that no one was hurt. This could have been so much worse, but he protected us. Even the man who we were unable to find last night has been located by the town police. He is fine, and we don't know yet whether he had anything to do with the fire, so let's be careful what we say or think."

He took a deep breath. "Cari is upstairs. If you lost your sleeping spot, go see Cari. She will tell you where to go and make sure you have some bedding. Many of you are going to have to sleep in the sanctuary. Just be sure to roll up your bedding and set it off to the side when you get up in the morning. And everybody else, don't bother people's stuff when it's in the sanctuary. I've got a guest room and a couch in the parsonage. Cari will be assigning some of the women and children to those spaces. So, if you need a place to go, see Cari."

The room remained strangely silent for a moment after he left; people were sort of frozen. Then a guy named Luke shouted, "Any pretty girls want to double up with me, that's cool." Only a few people laughed, but it broke the tension, and people started to mill about.

Maggie went back to her room, lay down, and opened her Bible, but then she just stared at the pages. She couldn't seem to make her eyes focus on the words. She desperately wanted Galen, but she didn't want to interrupt his work day, especially after he'd been up all night.

Unable to read, she tried to fall asleep. That didn't work either. She decided to go look for Harmony. The halls were mostly empty, and she made her way to the sanctuary. Little clusters of people were sitting around, some drinking coffee, a few playing cards on the floor. A little girl was dancing by the altar. There was no music.

Maggie moved on to the kitchen. There were more people there, but no Harmony. She did see Jackie. She sat down beside her. "Have you seen Harmony?" she asked.

Jackie snickered.

"What?" Maggie asked. "What's so funny?"

"I have no idea where she is, but I can tell you who she's with."

Maggie was stumped, and a little jealous at the idea of Harmony hanging out with someone else. "Who?"

Jackie looked at her like she was stupid. "Levi, of course. Those two are like teenagers in heat."

"Oh," Maggie said. That was certainly news to her, and she was legitimately concerned for Harmony. "Anybody know anything about this Levi guy?"

"Anybody know anything about anybody?" Jackie asked.

"OK, well, if you see her, will you tell her I was looking for her?" Maggie asked.

"Yep," Jackie answered, without looking up.

Maggie decided she needed a book. She headed to the church library, which was actually a doorless closet with bookshelves. Someone before Maggie's time, someone named Erika, had made it her mission to try to make it a real library, and apparently, the closet boasted a decent collection of quality literature. Maggie wasn't sure she could tell the difference between quality and junk, but she figured she'd just pick one with a flashy cover.

As she approached the library, she thought it was odd that no one had been assigned to sleep in there yet. She flipped on the light and what she saw scared the boots right off her. She'd found Harmony all right. And Levi.

"Harmony!" Maggie exclaimed, sounding too much like a pious old lady.

Harmony flopped off Levi's lap and scrambled to pull her shirt back on. Levi just sat there looking proud. "Maggie, you scared me!" Harmony said.

"I scared you? You guys are the ones crouching in the dark." Maggie gave Levi a disgusted look and then turned back to her friend. "Can I talk to you for a sec?"

"Sure," Harmony said, getting up. She gave Levi a quick peck and then said, "Be right back sugar," in a voice Maggie didn't care for.

As soon as they were out in the hall, Maggie said, "Are you sure about this?"

"About what?" Harmony asked.

"About him! How well do you know this guy?"

"Oh I don't know, about as well as you know G."

"That's different!" Maggie snapped.

"How?"

And before Maggie could stop herself, she spat out, "Because G's not homeless!"

Harmony looked as if she'd been slapped. "Well excuse me, Miss High Standards, in case you haven't noticed, we're *all* homeless." Harmony turned and stomped back into the library.

"Harmony, wait," Maggie began, but she was gone.

Maggie couldn't stand it anymore. She drove to Galen's.

She found him with his head under a hood, and again, the sight of him took her breath away. He looked up. "Hey!" he said, not sounding all that surprised to see her.

"Hey, how tired are you?" Maggie asked.

"Actually," he said, chuckling, "I was just thinking about taking a nap, but then I'd be up all night."

"Well, I tried to take a nap, but I couldn't either. But I also can't sit around that shelter all day without my bathroom. I'm going nuts."

By the look on Galen's face, she had sounded snarkier than she'd meant to.

"Well, you're welcome to hang out here. It will take me another hour or so to finish this up, but then I can hang out if you want."

"Awesome," she said, and meant it. "Until then, do you mind if I use your computer?"

"Of course not. Help yourself."

She headed upstairs and opened the door to find Eddie asleep on Galen's pillow. When she shut the door, the noise woke him up, but he only raised his head to look at her, gave her a salutatory wag, and then laid his head down again.

Seeing her was becoming less and less a special occasion. She couldn't have that, so she ran to the bed and leapt on it, burying her face in Eddie's fur. She laid there snuggling him for a bit, and then, when she felt herself falling asleep, she didn't fight it.

Chapter 28
Galen

Galen finished up on the Volkswagen and headed upstairs. He was incredibly curious about what Maggie wanted with his computer, but he didn't find her at his desk. He found her asleep on his bed, his bedspread folded over onto her legs, her face pressed into Eddie's side. His heart was overcome with affection. He felt as though he was looking at his family.

He took a hot shower and then tried to get dressed in his tiny bathroom. This was problematic, and he rapped his elbow on the door jamb hard enough to shake the floor. He expected that would wake folks up, but when he opened the door, Eddie only opened one eye to give him a dirty look. Maggie didn't budge. *Well this is going to be a fun visit*, he thought.

He jiggled his computer mouse to see what she'd been up to, but there was no evidence she'd even used the thing. He decided to let her sleep and headed out to get some lunch.

When he returned, she was seated at the computer, and for that he was grateful. "Hey, I got some cold cuts and bread, if you want a sand..." he stopped talking when he saw what she was looking at on the computer screen. Levi's obnoxious face was staring back at him from his own screen, and something close to rage filled his stomach. Galen wasn't used to this much anger, and he didn't like the feeling. "You're using my computer to look up that guy?" Galen said, trying not to raise his voice.

Maggie turned to look at him wide-eyed. When she saw his face, she jumped up and practically ran to him. She put her hands on his cheeks, "No, no, no, Galen, it's not what you think. Shh ..." she was talking to him in a voice close to what she used to talk to Eddie. He didn't know if that was a good or a bad thing, but his heart rate slowed a bit. "Harmony is seeing him. I don't think it's good. I was trying to find some dirt on him so I can talk her out of it."

"Oh." *Well aren't I the horse's butt?* "Sorry. I thought …" he stopped, unsure of what to say next. He was relieved and embarrassed at the same time. This was way more emotion than he was used to.

"I know what you thought, and I'm telling you, I am *not* interested in Levi. I'm only interested in *you.*"

Wait. What? Did I just hear that right? She was still so close to him, standing right in front of him, her hands on his face. *Did she really just say that?*

As if sensing what he had just thought, she slid her hands down to rest on his shoulders, which was considerably less intimate, but still pretty awesome. She was looking at him. He was dumbfounded. *Am I supposed to kiss her? Am I supposed to say something? Am I just supposed to stand here like an idiot?* He cleared his throat, and then was instantly embarrassed. It was a lot like coughing in her face. She didn't seem to mind though. She was just standing there looking at him.

"Oh," he said again.

She giggled. "Sorry," she said, and he could have sworn she was flirting, "is that news to you?"

He had an urge to clear his throat again, but stopped himself. "Yes."

"Sorry," she said again. "I told you. I'm a mess. But, this mess is very much in love with you, so you're kind of stuck with me."

It was immense elation and immense relief at the same time. He was suddenly floating in the sky, afraid to look down, but he also felt a supernatural peace flood through him. He wasn't sure whether to laugh or cry, so he kissed her. And she kissed him back this time. And it was the best kiss he'd ever had in his life. And all the pain of a difficult marriage, all the pain of an embarrassing divorce, all the pain of wanting a Maggie who didn't want him back—it all just melted to nothing in the warmth of that kiss.

Chapter 29

Monday morning, Maggie woke to a terrible racket. Pounding and hollering and something that sounded like a bulldozer pushing on her pillow. She rolled over and looked down at a terrified Amy perched on the edge of her bunk. "Good morning," Maggie said.

"Good morning," she said.

"Any idea what that awful banging is?" Maggie asked.

"No."

"Don't be scared," Maggie said, jumping down and reaching for her clothes. "Let's go check it out. It's probably something wonderful and exciting."

Maggie was just trying to make Amy feel better, but she couldn't have been more correct. The two women followed the banging outside and then blinked in the brilliant morning sunshine. It took several moments to figure out what was going on, and then Maggie gasped.

There were people everywhere, most of them men, and many of them wearing hardhats. An excavator was scooping up and carrying off what was left of the addition. A truck dumped a load of lumber, and there was another crash as snow flew into the air.

"What is happening?" Maggie's new roomie asked.

"I guess we're building something? Let's go find out." Maggie didn't see Cari anywhere, but she did see Pastor. He was standing between two official-looking men.

He saw her staring at him and called out, "Good morning, ladies! Quite the spectacle, huh?"

"I guess so," Maggie said. She walked toward him, and Amy followed. "What exactly is it?"

"Well, apparently, we're building a new addition, a bigger, better addition. And this time we're actually using plans." He nodded toward two men looking at blueprints.

"Did we win the lottery?" Maggie asked. Pastor sort of scowled, but Maggie thought it a reasonable question.

"Nope. The fire made national news. A megachurch in Houston heard about our plight. And they hired these contractors to fix our church."

Whoah. "And it's happening this fast?"

"Yep. God can be quite speedy when he wants to be."

"Wow."

"I've got to go back inside," Amy said. "I'm cold."

Maggie started to say goodbye to her, but Amy was already too far away to hear her over all the noise. Maggie stayed to watch. Many of the church men were standing around, some even looking as if they wanted to help. She herself had the urge to put on some work boots and gloves, but of course, she had nothing of the sort. And even in the most appropriate apparel, she would still be fairly useless. She considered offering the construction workers free haircuts, but then she remembered her bathroom and became sad all over again. They could build a new church; it could even have shiny, new spacious restrooms, but her weird little salon would still be gone.

Maggie headed back inside to sulk some more. As she walked past the office, Cari flagged her down. "G called. He wants you to call him back."

Maggie went into the office and dialed the familiar number.

"Hullo?" he said.

"Hey."

"Hey you, I was wondering if you had any plans for New Year's Eve."

Her chest tightened. "Of course not."

"Well," he said, "I was wondering if you wanted to go to a party with me?"

"A party?"

"Well, yeah, a party, but nothing too intense. Just a bunch of eating and drinking and being merry."

"Who?"

"You mean who will be there?"

"Yeah."

He paused. "Well, uh, you won't know any of them, but there's a few friends from high school. The party is actually at my cousin's house. He's actually my third cousin. But, anyway, I won't know some of the people, but ... look, if you don't want to go, that's cool."

But she knew it wasn't. "Yeah, of course, I'd love to go. Do I need to dress up?"

"Nope."

"OK, what about curfew?"

"I'll have you back in time."

They hung up and Maggie commenced to panic. A party.

Wednesday night came quickly. She changed three times, and then put the first outfit back on. She put makeup on for the first time since Massachusetts, but then decided to wash it all off. She curled her hair and put on some lip balm.

Galen was waiting for her when she left Bible study. He looked great, and her panic eased off a bit.

"You OK?" he asked, as they were walking to the truck.

"Sure. Just, don't ... I don't mean to be all clingy and needy, but just don't leave me alone, OK?"

He took her hand. "I won't. I promise."

The party was only a few miles away. His cousin lived in a gorgeous, cozy log cabin on the Benton Road. There were probably only about 20 to 25 people there, but it felt like more because the cabin was so small.

Galen guided her around, introducing her to people. She noticed that everybody seemed to really like Galen. Of course, this didn't really surprise her. But she noticed that he never offered much information about her. Just her name. He didn't call her his girlfriend, and he didn't say where she lived, or what she did. She started to wonder if he was ashamed of her.

It was only a few minutes after eight when Galen said, "You want to go home?"

"No, I'm OK."

He smiled. "Don't lie."

"Sorry," she said, and meant it. "I'm not trying to be a stick in the mud. It just comes naturally to me."

"That's OK, really. Come on, let's get you back to church before you turn into a pumpkin."

Chapter 30

The addition was a massive undertaking. The church was more than doubling in size. It was a busy place. People were always bustling about. It seemed as though there were more people than ever sleeping at the church, but this might have just been because of the lack of actual beds. One afternoon, Maggie actually stepped over someone napping in the hallway.

Because she was focused on not stepping on him, she almost smashed into Skylar, who was coming down the hall toward her. Skylar was a thirty-something, self-proclaimed recovering hippie. Maggie had cut her hair soon after Skylar had first arrived at the church.

"Hey!" Skylar exclaimed. "I was just looking for you!"

"Sorry, I'm not doing haircuts right now. My bathroom was lost in the fire."

"I know, but can't we just use another bathroom?"

Maggie sighed. She couldn't help it. She was annoyed. She had lost her salon. Couldn't these people understand that? Couldn't they just give her some space and let her breathe a little? *I don't even like people. Why on earth do I live in a homeless shelter?*

"Please?" Skylar asked, her eyebrows raised.

"I'm sorry, Skylar, I just don't think so," Maggie said, trying to move past her.

But Skylar took a step back. "Maggie, I don't think you understand."

Maggie stopped. "What do you mean?"

"You don't know what your haircuts do. You can't just stop."

"What my haircuts *do*?"

"Yes. Your haircuts change things. Mine changed things for me. People looked at me different after. You gave me the courage to apply for a job.... I didn't get it, but still. You did that."

Maggie didn't know what to say.

But she moved her salon to the bathroom that had the showers. It was a much busier place, and she always felt she was in someone's way. And she was on her own. Harmony was still mad at her, wouldn't speak to her, and certainly wouldn't be her bodyguard. Fewer people came to see her there. They were frequently running low on hot water. The few community members who trickled in for cuts never came back. Boy, how she missed her old bathroom. How she missed Harmony.

She was however, getting to spend a lot of time with Galen, and that was a good thing. They ate good food, snuggled a lot, and watched a lot of sports. She couldn't believe how sweet he was to her. He seemed to actually find her interesting. He listened to her when she talked and laughed at her jokes. It was all very strange. But she liked it.

One night, during another *Reba* episode, he said, "You know, maybe while you've got some downtime, you could pursue licensing."

"Downtime? Is that what this is?"

"Well, you used to sort of have a full-time job, right? Now it's more like part-time? And you don't seem exactly thrilled with the way things are going."

She knew he meant well, but she was still annoyed with the direction of this conversation. "So I can hang my license in the shower room?"

"Look," he sighed, "I'm not pressuring you or anything. I'm trying to be encouraging. You're obviously talented. Maybe you would like to work in a real salon?"

She thought she understood then what he was getting at, and she became rampantly defensive. "Galen, does it actually bother you that I live at a homeless shelter?"

He looked at her as if she had lizards crawling out of her ears. "Are you nuts? Of course not."

"Well, then why are you trying to push me into a job? I had a job."

He sighed and pulled her closer to him. "Honey, I'm not pushing you to anything. When you used to work out of your little makeshift salon, you had a twinkle in your eye. I don't see the twinkle anymore. I'm just trying to figure out how to give it back to you." He kissed her on the forehead, and she realized she was being a nitwit. She nuzzled into his chest and thanked God for the zillionth time for this man.

"I'm sorry, Galen. Thank you for putting up with me."

His chest moved up and down with a chuckle. "No problem. I love putting up with you. And really, I don't care if you want to live in a church for the rest of your life."

Chapter 31

Despite how grumpy she'd been with Galen, after letting his words marinate for a while, she realized he was right. Why on earth wouldn't she want to be licensed? So one Saturday afternoon, she told him as much and asked to use his computer to research the process. Turns out, it was all fairly simple, and of course, Galen offered to help her with the testing and licensing fees, which were significant. The next exam was in Brewer in two weeks.

That night at Bible study, the Mayor surprised them with another visit. The worship team belted out their set with their usual gusto, and Maggie couldn't help but watch the poor man. He looked so uncomfortable. He sat only three rows from the front, so he really didn't even have much to look at, but still, he looked as if he was sitting in a tank full of spiders.

After the worship team's set, Pastor took a microphone and asked if anyone had any praises they would like to share. He didn't do this very often, and Maggie presumed he was doing it now for the Mayor's benefit.

Beau volunteered to go first. He wanted to praise God that he had received a letter from his granddaughter. Beau and his granddaughter hadn't spoken for years, and his daughter had forbidden contact between the two of them, so a letter was significant. Beau got choked up at the end, so Maggie did too.

Next was Amber. She wanted to thank God for her new job as a dishwasher at the diner. She said she hoped to save up enough money to get her own place.

Next was José. He had a praise and a prayer request. He had decided to quit smoking. For real this time. Next was Carl. He either hadn't listened to José or simply didn't care. He announced that he had "finally" received his disability check, and had purchased three cartons of cigarettes, and he was willing to share with anyone in need. Maggie, knowing how scarce cigarettes could be for some, recognized this for the generous offer it was, but Pastor couldn't get the mic out of Carl's hands fast enough.

Maggie snuck a look at the Mayor. The spiders were apparently crawling up his pant legs. Pastor announced then that the Mayor would be speaking. He gave him a resounding intro, which included thanking him for his support of the church.

"Thank you, Daniel," he said, taking the mic, "that's mighty kind of you." He smiled, or at least tried to. "I came here tonight to talk to you about some difficult things, but I wanted you all to know what's going on. Daniel tells me that this place can be quite the rumor mill, so I wanted to set the record straight." As he talked, he fluctuated between looking at the floor in front of his feet and looking at the back wall. Maggie was surprised at his lack of comfort with public speaking. *Maybe I should run for public office*, she thought.

"The arson investigator has found evidence that the tragic fire of December 26th was set intentionally. The police have arrested a suspect. He was staying here that night. His name is Aaron St. Lawrence. He started a fire in a trash can, and claims that it was never supposed to be as bad as it was. He said he was just trying to get everyone out of the church, not trying to burn the building down. He seems to be sincerely sorry. Mr. St. Lawrence claims that he was paid to start the fire. He claims he was paid by Lance Pouliot, Mattawooptock's Code Enforcement Officer." The Mayor paused to allow the collective gasp, and Maggie heard a few expletives fired from the back row.

"But wait," he continued. "We have no evidence that this is true. At this point, it is one man's word against another. Police will continue to investigate, but I wanted to let you all know that Mr. Pouliot has resigned from his position. In addition, excuse the pun ..." The Mayor stopped to laugh, but no one else joined him. Then Pastor gave him a charity chuckle. "So, in addition, you shouldn't have to worry about codes ever again. The contractors have asked for all the codes, and this new building will be compliant. So, if you were ever concerned, don't be. Thank you for your time, and when the time comes, I would appreciate your votes."

He sat down, and Pastor stood up to take his place. Pastor started clapping, and a few people joined in, but it was a pretty pathetic offering. Pastor thanked the Mayor again, and then gave a short sermon on forgiveness. How appropriate.

Chapter 32

A week later, Maggie found herself recruiting volunteers. The licensing exam included both a written portion and a practical portion. Maggie had done some studying, with the help of Galen and his internet connection, and she wasn't worried about the written portion. She was, however, a little concerned about the practical part. She had taken to just sort of following her muse when it came to cutting people's hair. Her methods weren't exactly textbook.

She had no trouble finding volunteers. Mothers were especially willing to volunteer their children. So, Maggie dove back into her work with a newfound gusto. She still missed her salon, but she realized that she had also missed all the people. Now that she was back to being busy, she was feeling better.

So, when, on her way to dinner, she noticed Cari carrying big boxes into the office, she sounded downright chipper when she asked, "What's all that?"

"Donations from a shoe store," Cari grunted as she dropped what looked to be a fairly heavy box in the middle of the office.

"Really?" Maggie asked. In her old life, shoes had been pretty exciting stuff. "Can I help?"

"You sure can," Cari said, still out of breath, "but don't get too excited."

"What do you mean? Why not?"

"Well, sometimes donations aren't really donations. Sometimes they're just a tax write-off. Come on, there's more boxes outside."

Is that where the crockpots came from? Maggie followed Cari to the door.

"Lift with your legs," Cari said as she grunted again. Maggie grabbed the last box, which was indeed heavy, and carried it into the office.

"There," Cari sighed, leaning on the pile of boxes. "Hand me those scissors," she panted, pointing at her desk with her chin. Then she deftly cut into the top box and opened it. And pulling out a layer of bubble wrap revealed what looked like ballet shoes. She pulled a package out and held it in front of Maggie's face like a dead mouse. "See? Ballet slippers. Just what every homeless man needs."

Maggie wasn't defeated though. "There's got to be something else. Why would they send us ballet shoes?" She dove into the box and started to dig, but sure enough, it was a homogeneous mix. All white. All ballet. Maggie didn't understand. She put her hands on her hips. "But why?" she asked Cari.

Cari shrugged. "Like I said. Write-off."

"What about that one?" Maggie asked.

Cari ripped into the next box. At least this one was more colorful. At first it appeared promising, but as Maggie inspected the box's contents, she saw that these weren't actually tennis shoes, or running shoes, or anything else useful. They were soccer cleats. Lots of colors, and lots of sizes, but all cleats. "At least these might work for the church softball team," Cari exclaimed and heaved them over to the other side of the room.

Maggie took the scissors and ripped into the third box. Flip-flops. "Well, that's not bad," Maggie declared.

"Yeah, except it's January, and there's two feet of snow outside."

"Good point. But I'm taking a pair for the showers."

"That might be wise." Cari heaved the box of flip-flops to the other side of her office, slamming it down on top of the cleats.

Dale appeared in the doorway, "Can I get my meds?"

Cari didn't even look at the clock. "Not time yet, Dale."

Maggie looked at him. He didn't look to be in good shape. "Please?... I really need them now, Cari."

Cari paused and looked up. "OK, do you want me to call your doctor?" Dale didn't answer. Instead, he collapsed, right there in the doorway. "Call 911," Cari said and rushed to his side.

Maggie dialed the number as Cari checked for a pulse and lowered her ear to Dale's mouth.

The operator answered. Maggie gave him the address. When he asked for the nature of the emergency, she didn't know what to say. She said, "Dale ... he just collapsed."

"His heart is beating," Cari said, and then she took a deep breath and tilted Dale's head back, opening his mouth at the same time. Then she was breathing into his mouth. One breath. Two. Maggie could see his chest rising.

The operator told Maggie that there was an ambulance on the way. She just stood there holding the phone, feeling useless, and silently thanking God that Cari was there. She knew she wouldn't be able to handle this. A crowd was starting to form around the office door. "Get back," Cari snapped between breaths, "give him some room."

"Come on, guys," Maggie tried to help, "back up. Give Dale some space. We don't want him to wake up to you all hanging over him. That's liable to give him a heart attack." No one laughed, but they did back up.

She heard the sirens, but it seemed an eternity between hearing the sirens and seeing the paramedics. When they did get there, they wasted no time. In a minute they had Dale hoisted onto the gurney and on his way to the hospital.

And then they all just stood there staring at the door. Even the kids were quiet. Maggie suddenly really missed Hershel. "We should pray," she said. No one said anything. "We should pray right now," she repeated, and she got down on her knees, right there in the lobby. And everyone got down on their knees with her. And they prayed for Dale.

Chapter 33

The next few days around the shelter were somber. The construction crew kept pounding away, and there was a steady murmur of discontented whispers in every corner, but that was pretty much it. On the second night Dale spent in the hospital, Pastor passed the microphone around to allow people to share praises. Maggie figured he did so to try to lighten the mood, to show people that God was still doing good things, but it sort of backfired.

The only person who stood up to share was Linda, who had finally, after many months of waitlist, received a housing voucher from the state. She, of course, was elated. Maggie felt genuine joy for her too, but then found she was alone in that sentiment, or close to it.

When Linda finished her testimony, no one clapped, and Maggie even heard a few muttered obscenities. People seemed angry, not joyous. Maggie realized there were probably many people in the room on the waitlist. And they were probably experiencing a range of emotions, from jealousy to anger to resentment to bitterness—all a long distance from joy. Maggie promised God to give Linda a big congratulatory hug before she left, even though that would take her a mile outside her comfort zone. But she was Linda's hairdresser after all.

Pastor preached on Nehemiah that night. Maggie had trouble focusing. But then, at one point, Dan mentioned how winter can be tough on people emotionally and psychologically, and it dawned on Maggie that she was sitting in a room where the majority of people probably suffered from Seasonal Affective Disorder. It was a wonder they were getting along as well as they were.

Maggie had actually grown content with her home there, but she also knew she was in the minority. Most people only saw the church as a waypoint or an emergency pit stop.

Most people wanted out, and they were only waiting for the pastor to stop talking so they could go sulk in their beds.

Finally, Pastor did stop talking. And Maggie was grateful that he skipped the altar call.

When she got back to her room, she found Harmony crying on her bed. The sound of it made her heart crack.

"Sweetie, what's wrong?" Maggie said, kneeling beside her bed. Harmony didn't answer, just sniffed. Maggie started rubbing her back. She gave her a few seconds to respond, but when she didn't, she said, "I know you're mad at me, Harmony, but I'm still your friend. Actually, I'm your sister, so let me help you. What's going on?"

Harmony rolled over then and choked out, "I'm sorry, Maggie. I shouldn't have been so mad at you. I just … I just love him … and he's … he's …"

"He's what, sweetie?"

"He's … gone!" Harmony pushed the last word out of her mouth as if it hurt her to say it.

"What do you mean, gone?"

"I mean, he didn't come to Bible study, so I went looking for him, and he's gone."

"Well, maybe he just went to the store or something. He's probably just playing hooky."

"No," Harmony sighed, rolling over onto her back. "He would have told me if he was going to the store. And I went to his bed, and all his stuff is gone. He's really gone. He left me."

Maggie didn't know what to say. She felt her heart fill with something close to hatred. Her instinct was to tell Harmony that this guy was a total loser and that Harmony was better off without him, but she felt the Holy Spirit tell her to just be quiet. So she was. She grabbed Harmony's hand instead, and held it tight.

Chapter 34

Maggie was just finishing up a color when Harmony let her know there was a young man waiting for her outside the bathroom. Relieved to get out of the steam for a minute, Maggie stepped out into the hallway to find Ethan waiting for her.

Ethan had been in and out of the shelter several times, but Maggie hadn't yet actually talked to him. But that didn't stop Ethan from seeming incredibly comfortable with her. He seemed to have his swagger on. "Hey, how'd you like to make this even sexier?" he asked, pointing to his head.

She couldn't help but laugh. That only encouraged him though. He took a step toward her. She took a step back. "I can give you a haircut, but I've got to finish up with Trixie first," she tried.

"No problem. I think you're worth the wait."

Because she didn't know what else to do, she turned and went back into the bathroom.

"Another appointment?" Trixie asked.

"Yeah, I guess," Maggie sighed. "Though I don't know if he wants a haircut or if he just wants me to touch his head. Do you know Ethan?"

Maggie felt Trixie shudder. "Yeah, he thinks he's something."

Maggie tried to take her time rinsing Trixie's hair, and when she finished, Ethan had disappeared. It was just as well. The construction crew was making even more noise than usual, and she was getting a headache. She headed to her room to lie down.

Predictably, Jackie was also lying on her bed, reading. "Hey, Jackie," Maggie said, heaving herself onto the top bunk.

"Reading," Jackie said.

Maggie ignored the hint. "Have you heard anything about Dale?"

"Nope," Jackie said, not looking up. "Still reading."

Maggie was quiet for a minute and then said, "Hey, Jackie? How come you never let me cut your hair?"

Jackie didn't respond.

"Hey, Jackie! Earth to Jackie!"

Jackie sighed. "I think this head is beyond repair."

Maggie looked at her. "Don't be ridiculous. We could color it, cut it, curl it, whatever you want."

"I just want to read."

"Fine," Maggie said, finally taking the hint. She rolled over to face the giraffe, and despite the banging, which was muffled a bit now, fell asleep.

About an hour later, Maggie woke up and rolled over to find Jackie sitting up on her own bunk, her legs dangling over the edge, staring at her.

"What?" Maggie asked, a little creeped out.

"Did you mean it?"

Maggie honestly couldn't remember what she'd said. "Mean what?"

"My hair?"

"Of course I can cut your hair, Jackie. What do you want me to do?"

Jackie looked almost sheepish. This was new. "I've always wished I was a redhead."

"OK, well, in this day and age, Jackie, we can do that," Maggie joked.

Jackie didn't laugh. "OK, what do we need to do?"

"Well, do you have a few bucks? We need to go get some color."

"I don't have a few bucks."

"OK, well, I do. Let's go," Maggie said, jumping off the bed.

Jackie didn't move. "Go where?"

"To the drugstore."

Jackie actually looked scared. Maggie tried to think of a time when Jackie had actually left the church. She couldn't remember one. Even when they all had gone to the mall, Jackie had stayed behind, claiming to hate malls.

"Jackie, when is the last time you left this property?"

Jackie didn't answer. "Can't you just go get the color for me?"

Maggie sighed. "I could, but don't you want to pick out your own color? It's your head."

Jackie seemed to chew on this for a few seconds. Then she put her book down and painstakingly climbed out of her bunk. "Let's go," she said, and headed for the door.

Considering it was still January, it was fairly warm out, almost 20 degrees. Maggie noticed, too late, that Jackie was wearing slippers. She started to ask her about it, but then thought better of it.

As they walked into Rite Aid, the clerk gave them a dirty look, but the two women ignored her. Maggie headed straight for the hair care aisle. She knew it well. Jackie followed, looking painfully uncomfortable.

Maggie stopped in front of the reds. "So, any of these flip your switch?"

Jackie frowned. "Why are there so many?"

"I don't know," Maggie said, "'cause there's lots of shades of red? I recommend choosing one with built-in highlights. That way, it will look more natural."

Jackie snorted. "You actually think you can make it look *real*?"

"Of course I can. Look who you're talking to. I'm a pro ... sort of."

Jackie stood staring, looking overwhelmed.

Maggie grabbed a promising box of Rich Auburn Blonde. "Is this too blond?"

Jackie looked at it as though it was a bomb about to go off. "Are you sure that stuff won't hurt my hair?"

Maggie laughed. She couldn't help it. It had never occurred to her that Jackie cared one iota about hair health. "Um, yeah, well, it's not very good for your hair. It's kind of harsh, I mean, it's a bunch of chemicals, but really, it'll be OK." Maggie paused, but when Jackie didn't respond, she continued, "I like this one, let's go."

"No," Jackie said emphatically, sounding more like the Jackie Maggie knew and loved. "This one," she said, grabbing a box of Cherry Crush.

Maggie felt her eyes get big. "Wow! That's really red."

"I know, I like it," Jackie said, and spun on her slippered feet toward the checkout.

"You sure do buy a lot of hair products," the snotty clerk offered, without making eye contact.

Maggie took her time counting out her seven dollars in change. "Yep, well, I do a lot of hair."

The clerk looked up then and raised an eyebrow. "Oh yeah? Why's that?"

"I do people's hair at the church up the road. You know, the shelter."

The clerk rolled her eyes and started to count the change. A younger woman at the next register chimed in though. "How much do you charge?"

"Nada," Maggie said. "I just do it out of the kindness of my heart ... but you'll have to stand for your shampoo."

The girl looked surprised. "Seriously? You'd do my hair too?"

"Sure," Maggie said, "come on over anytime. My name is Maggie. Someone will find me for you. I think you'd look great with some bangs. You have beautiful eyes."

Clerk number one handed Maggie her bag and a healthy dose of disdain, while clerk number two muttered, "Thanks."

"No problem. See you soon."

Chapter 35

The whole church was talking about Jackie's hair. Not only could she pull off Cherry Crush, she was *rocking* it. Soft layers fell around her shoulders and seemed to bounce when she walked. Maggie kept catching her playing with it, probably when she thought no one was watching.

It had been three days since the paramedics had taken Dale away, and still, no word. Cari was sick, so the entire church was sort of hanging on by a thread. Everyone was staggering around in confusion.

Maggie figured Pastor had gone to see him, but she could never find Pastor to ask him how Dale was. After Bible study Friday night, she tried to talk to him, but he was mobbed at the altar by people with problems. She considered waiting her turn, but Ethan was in the line, and she couldn't make herself do it.

So, Saturday morning, she called Galen from the church office.

"Hello?"

"Let's go see Dale."

"Well, good morning to you too. How are you, sweetheart?"

"I'm good. I want to go see Dale. Want to go with me?"

"Uh, sure, I'll be right over."

It took Galen longer than usual, so Maggie gave up waiting at the door. Eventually, he showed up at her room. "You ready?" he asked, and then, noticing Jackie, who was putting clean laundry away, added, "Whoa! Did you get a new roommate, Maggs?"

Maggie and Jackie both smiled. "Nope. Same old crotchety me. But *Maggs* here gave me a new do. What do you think?"

"I think you look great."

"Thanks, G," Jackie said through a mostly toothless grin, and turned back to her laundry.

"Yep, I'm ready," Maggie said, and led the way to the lobby.

After climbing into the truck and giving Eddie an exorbitant number of kisses, Maggie said, "Thanks for this. I'm just really worried. No one seems to know anything about Dale, and I can't seem to pencil myself in to Pastor's schedule to ask him."

"Do we even know where Dale is?"

"I'm assuming that he's right in Mattawooptock? At the hospital ... isn't he?"

Galen shrugged, "I don't know. If it was serious, they would've taken him to Bangor or Portland. Does Cari know where he is?"

"Probably, but she's sick."

"Oh no, Cari never gets sick. What's wrong with her?"

"I dunno. I think just a cold? I'm not sure."

"Well, maybe we should be bringing her soup instead of stalking Dale?"

Maggie laughed despite herself. "Fine. Good idea, we'll bring her soup on the way back, OK? But I'm really worried about Dale."

"OK," Galen conceded, and drove for several miles in silence. Then he asked, "How's the practicing going?"

"You mean hair?"

"No, free throws. Yes, I mean hair."

"Oh, it's good I guess. I think I'm ready. I mean, I guess I have to be ready. The test is Monday. Oh shoot, I completely forgot." Maggie heaved a big sigh. "I hate to ask you for anything else, but I need some stuff for the exam."

"Sure, like what?"

"Like a head, and a hand, or at least a finger —"

"A head?" Galen interrupted.

"Yeah, like a mannequin head. And some other stuff too. Like a good curling iron. I'm sorry."

"No worries, I'm happy to help. You're a good investment. But as for the head, can't you just bring Jackie?"

"I don't think so. I'm going to stand out enough as it is. Don't want to show up with a human mannequin too."

"How are you going to stand out?" Galen asked, pulling into the hospital parking lot.

"Because I don't know what I'm doing half the time."

"Well, you certainly did great work on Jackie. She looks like a new woman."

Chapter 36

"Hi there," Galen said with what sounded like fake cheerfulness. "We're looking for Dale Prescott. We believe he was brought here after a heart attack a few days ago?" Galen asked the helpful-looking woman behind the counter at Mattawooptock General Hospital.

"Three days ago," Maggie tried to help, as the woman pounded on her keyboard.

"Yes, Mr. Prescott is in room 311."

The hospital was tiny, yet they still had trouble finding room 311. The building was laid out a lot like their church: nonsensically. Finally, they found him. He had his own room and was propped up looking fairly healthy after all. "Hi, Dale," Galen said as they strode in, "how are you feeling?"

"Well, if it isn't my favorite twosome! What are you two doing here?"

Galen sat down in the only chair and said, "Well, Maggie here was worried about you, so we thought we'd come check on you." Maggie felt embarrassed all of a sudden and really wished she had a chair. She felt like a giant standing next to a sitting Galen and fully reposed Dale.

"Well, I'm gonna live, I guess. Had myself a heart attack. Guess I should a seen it coming. Done some hard livin', these old veins. They say I can leave if I pass my stress test. I can do it—haven't smoked in three days. Though maybe I should stay in here so I stay a nonsmoker. I can taste my food now."

Dale's tone was downright morbid, leaving his visitors momentarily speechless. After a few awkward seconds, Galen asked, "So the food's good then?"

Dale practically snarled, "Oh yeah, steak and bacon every night."

Maggie could see Galen was uncomfortable, and felt guilty for dragging him there. She suddenly felt as though

Dale was a stranger to her. She *lived* with the man, but how well did she really know him? *Is a two-minute visit ruder than no visit at all?*

"So what are you watching?" Galen asked, turning his chair around, which put his back to Dale and his face to the TV. It didn't really matter; Dale wasn't looking at him anyway.

"*Star Trek* ... I've seen 'em all, but it's been a while."

Galen nodded, "Oh yeah, isn't this the one where we meet Spock's parents?"

Dale grunted. "Yep, that guy there isn't even an alien. He's just fakin' it. Even his antennas are fake."

Galen nodded as if this all made sense. Without turning away from the TV, he said in a strange semi-robotic voice, "Love is illogical."

Dale snorted approvingly.

Maggie looked at the stranger in the chair. *What on earth?*

The two men watched *Star Trek* in silence, and Maggie grew more uncomfortable and markedly bored. She wished again for a chair and opted to perch on one of Galen's knees instead. She was worried this might annoy him, but he didn't even seem to notice. They watched the rest of the episode, including commercials, in silence.

As soon as the credits rolled, however, Galen hopped up and said, "Well, Dale, I'm sure glad you're OK. You gave us quite a scare. Is there anything we can get for you?"

Dale looked at Galen then, and his gray eyes looked incredibly sad. "Nah, I'm good," he said, and returned his gaze to the TV.

"Can I pray with you before we go?" Galen asked.

Dale laughed, but it was humorless. "No thanks, that's my favorite part of being here—being away from all that baloney. And I'm only calling it baloney 'cause of the lady."

Galen nodded, seemingly unsurprised. "I understand, but you know Dale, you might be alive because of prayer. When you went to the hospital, your church went to their knees for you."

Dale, without looking away from the TV, said, "Maybe they shouldn't have."

Maggie was quiet all the way back to the truck, but then she couldn't hold it in anymore. "I don't understand. What's wrong with him?"

Galen looked a little annoyed, which annoyed her, because he had been so unannoyed with Dale. He sighed and said, "Honey, he's got a lot going on. We have no idea what sorts of mental health issues he's facing, or what meds they've got him on. He's probably going through extreme nicotine withdrawals. That can make you crazy. And he's recognizing that he could die, at any time, and he's not sure what would happen to him if he does. That's all pretty scary stuff."

Everything Galen had said made sense, but she still felt as though there was something else, something simple, something obvious. After a few minutes, she said, "We should find Hershel."

Galen sighed again. She couldn't see his eyes, but she suspected he had rolled them. "Honey, you can't fix everything. Sometimes you've just got to leave it to God."

Chapter 37

Maggie had no trouble finding a seat at church that night. *Where is everybody?* she wondered, but then Steve, wearing his AC/DC shirt again, got up to make some announcements. And when he prayed, he spent a good few minutes praying that God would "heal our sick brothers and sisters" and "stop this bug from spreading to the rest of us."

The sermon, about the patience of Job, was short. Pastor didn't look so good.

After closing things out with a rambunctious version of "He Reigns," Galen joined Maggie in exiting the sanctuary.

"Can I walk you to your truck?" she asked, leaning into him flirtatiously.

"Sure," he said, putting his arm around her shoulders. "Hey, you want me to get you a motel room for a few nights? We don't want you to be sick for your test."

"Nah, I'll be OK," Maggie said. "I eat my veggies."

Galen sighed as he held the door open for her. "OK, well, if you're all practiced up, maybe you should stop giving haircuts for a while. Limit your physical contact with everyone."

"OK, will do," she said, and then gave him a kiss. Her weak knees caught her by surprise. *Shouldn't I be used to that by now?* "Have a good night, Galen. Give my little buddy a big hug and kiss."

On the way back to her room, Maggie heard an abundance of sneezing, sniffing, and coughing. And she could hear Harmony coughing before she even got to her room. As she walked in, she met Jackie walking out, carrying a pillow and blanket.

"Where are you going?"

"I'm going to sleep in the hall. That chick is coughing directly up at me. And Amy's not much better. You might want to do the same."

Against Jackie's recommendation, Maggie went into her room. She didn't want to get sick, but she also didn't want to sleep in the hall.

Harmony looked as if she might be dying. Her hair was wet with sweat, and she looked pale and miserable.

"Oh sweetie, are you OK? Can I get you some water or something?"

Harmony coughed again. "That would be great," she whispered, and coughed.

"How about you Amy? Water?"

Amy nodded and whispered, "Thanks."

Maggie headed toward the kitchen, and encountered several people sleeping in the halls. At first she thought Jackie wasn't alone in her germ-avoidance methods, but then she realized that some of the hall-sleepers were coughing too, and assumed they had been kicked out of their rooms. She suddenly wished that Dale *wouldn't* come home right now. He was much safer where he was. She trotted down the familiar stairs to the kitchen, and as she rounded the corner to head for the glasses cupboard, she smacked right into Hershel.

"Hershel!" she squealed. She had the urge to throw her arms around him, but her inhibitions squashed it. "What are you doing here?"

"Well, I'm homeless. What are you doing here?" He sounded considerably less excited to see her.

She wasn't sure if he was trying to be funny, so she laughed. "When did you get back?"

"Just now, actually. I picked a heck of a time too, didn't I? Looks like the plague is sweeping through here."

"Yep, watch yourself."

"You too, toots," he said, and headed up the stairs.

She wasn't surprised at how happy she was to see him, but he didn't seem that excited to see her, and that hurt her a little. As she filled up the water glasses, it occurred to her, or rather, the Holy Spirit whispered to her, that something must have gone wrong for Hershel to be back at the shelter. It's not as if he had come back by choice.

She brought the water back to the girls, and Harmony asked her if she had any Tylenol or ibuprofen. She didn't, but she headed to the office to see if there was any there.

Of course, there was no one in the office. It was dark and locked up. So, she headed over to the parsonage.

A woman Maggie recognized, but didn't know by name, answered the door. She didn't look impressed to see Maggie. Maggie started to feel really tired.

"Hey," Maggie said. "Sorry to bother you, but there was no one in the church office. I was wondering if Pastor had any ibuprofen or Tylenol, something to help with fever? Maybe even some NyQuil?"

"Pastor's sleeping."

She wasn't sure how this could be true. Bible study had ended only minutes ago, but she also didn't want to argue with this woman, who had apparently designated herself the parsonage's bouncer. "OK, thanks anyway. Good night."

She walked back to the church, and, stepping over a few legs on the way, found Jenny sleeping in the hall. "Jenny," she whispered.

"Yeah? You don't have to whisper. I'm not sleeping." She coughed.

"Hey? Can I use your cell phone? I'm going to call Galen and ask him if he has any drugs."

"Drugs?" Jenny partially sat up.

"No, like Tylenol or ibuprofen."

"Sorry, I don't have any minutes left."

"OK, do you know anyone else who has a phone?"

"Nope." Jenny rolled over. She had obviously lost interest in Maggie's mission.

Maggie sighed. She didn't know anyone else with a phone. She decided she would just drive to Galen's, but she would have to hustle to make it back before curfew.

Despite being fairly confident in their relationship, she still felt like a stalker when she got to Galen's home. He lived over a garage. There was no doorbell. *How do I knock on a door, when there's an entire garage in the way?* She stood there, perplexed. Then she took a few steps back and looked up, even though there was absolutely nothing useful to look at. She thought about walking around to the side of the building his apartment was on, but what were the chances of him having a window open in January?

She heard Eddie bark. This made her smile, alone in the darkness. She was thinking about hollering Galen's name, when the door to the garage opened. Eddie bounded out past Galen's legs.

Momentarily ignoring Eddie, she said "Hi!" to Galen in a high-pitched voice that embarrassed her. Eddie jumped up and punched her in the stomach with both front paws.

"Hey," he said, "change your mind about the motel?"

"No, but people are really sick. Harmony's got a fever. I was wondering if you have any Tylenol or ibuprofen?"

He scratched his chin. "I don't think so. I'll go check. Come on in."

She followed him inside, and up the stairs. Eddie continued to jump on her, punching her in the butt as she headed up the stairs.

Galen rummaged through his medicine cabinet and then came out holding a small bottle. He shook it, apparently decided its contents were questionable, and momentarily wrestled with the childproof cap. He looked inside, then looked at her and declared, "There's only three left." Then he held the bottle out for her to see, but she couldn't see anything in the dim light.

"Oh, well, that's better than nothing. Thanks. Enough for Harmony and Amy at least."

"Well, not really. You might want to stop at Rite Aid and get some more."

"I would love to do that, and would have done that without bothering you, but of course, I have no money."

"Oh right, sorry." He handed her the bottle and headed to his dresser, presumably to find her some money.

"You don't have to give me any more money, Galen. It's not your problem."

"No, it's really OK. I'll take it out of my tithe." He laughed. "Here," he said, handing her two twenties. Then he walked past her toward the kitchenette.

"Wow, that's a lot. How much do you think ibuprofen costs?"

"Well, I figured you could get some Nyquil. That's got Tylenol in it, and will help with all the other junk as well. Here," he said, handing her a box of plastic spoons. "You can dose as many people as you want. Give the alcoholics the ibuprofen though."

She took the spoons. "How do I know who the alcoholics are?"

Galen sighed and rubbed his head. "I have no idea. Where is Pastor?"

"Sleeping, apparently. I think he might be sick too."

"OK, well, I guess you just have to ask them. If someone falls off the wagon tonight, it's probably not going to be your fault." He stopped talking and just looked at her.

"OK, then, I'll get out of your hair. Thanks," she said, playfully wagging the spoons at him. "Another jewel in your crown for this."

"Thanks, but I'm pretty sure that's not how it works."

Turns out forty dollars wasn't as much as she thought. It bought four bottles of Nyquil and a small bottle of no-name-brand ibuprofen.

There was a new woman behind the Rite Aid counter. She raised an eyebrow at Maggie, and said, "Can I see your ID?"

You've got to be kidding me. "I didn't bring in my ID. I just brought the cash."

"Can I see your ID?"

Maggie sighed. "Yeah, I'll be right back." Leaving the meds on the counter, she ran out to the car and found her driver's license.

"Massachusetts?" the woman re-raised the same obnoxious eyebrow.

Maggie wanted to tell her that she desperately needed to groom that thing, but instead said, "Yes."

"You came all the way from Mass to stock up on NyQuil?"

"Look, I'm kind of in a hurry."

The girl didn't move. "Why are you in such a hurry to buy four bottles of NyQuil?"

What on earth? Is this girl an undercover narcotics officer or something?

On the verge of a panic attack, Maggie said, "Look, I'm homeless. I live at the homeless shelter. Everybody there is sick. I'm trying to be a good person. But if I miss curfew and get locked out of the church, I am going to be really upset." As she spoke, her volume gradually increased, so that "upset" came out in a shrieky crescendo.

Maggie never knew whether it was the homelessness or the crescendo that scared the Rite Aid woman, but that was definitely fear on her face. And she rang Maggie up in record time.

"$38.72."

"Thanks."

When Maggie got back to the church, the clock on her dash read 8:42. She knew she had cut it close, but she also wondered if there was anyone healthy enough to lock the doors.

She stopped at the first person she found awake. "Hey, Sunny," she whispered, "Galen bought us some NyQuil, want some?"

"Sure, who is Galen?" Sunny asked, sitting up.

Maggie chuckled, "G ... never mind. Do you want some?"

"Of course."

Maggie handed her a spoon, and, as she was unwrapping the extra layer of plastic from the bottle, Sunny coughed directly into her face.

"Sorry," Sunny said, after she'd finished hacking.

Maggie tried to smile, and poured some NyQuil into Sunny's trembling spoon.

Just before the spoon entered Sunny's mouth, Maggie snapped, "Wait!"

"What?!" Sunny asked, sloshing most of the NyQuil off the spoon into her lap.

"Sorry, I was just supposed to ask if you're an alcoholic."

Sunny cackled, and then coughed again, but this time she covered her mouth. "Of course. Isn't everyone?"

Maggie was stumped for a few seconds. Then she said, "No, I mean, are you in recovery?"

Sunny laughed again. "Oh, of course not. Don't be ridiculous ... So can I have the medicine now?"

"I guess."

"Well, can my spoon get a refill?"

Maggie sighed and acquiesced.

Sunny swallowed, shuddered a bit at the taste, and asked for another. Then she lay back down. "Thank you."

"You're welcome," Maggie said, and moved on.

Maggie gave out NyQuil till she'd dirtied all her spoons. Then she went to the kitchen, washed the spoons, and then went for another round. At some point during this, she realized she was pretty much begging to get sick. But then she figured God would probably protect her, since she was doing his work.

Chapter 38

When she got to breakfast the next morning, she saw Hershel and Dale seated next to each other. She was wondering if she had somehow time traveled in her sleep, but then focused on the person offering her bacon. "Yes, please!" she said, excited. She had forgotten it was Sunday.

She filled her tray and then went to join Hershel and Dale. She sat down opposite them and didn't say anything.

"Good morning, little lady," Hershel said. Dale sort of half-smiled, bacon hanging out of his mouth.

"Good morning," Maggie answered.

And then the three of them sat there eating together in silence, as if nothing had happened, as if Dale had never almost died and Hershel hadn't just materialized. Maggie couldn't help but marvel at how truly strange the moment was, but she went with it. They all finished their coffee, and when the men went upstairs, Maggie followed.

She didn't sit with them in the sanctuary though. She drew the line there. She found Harmony near the front and slid in beside her. "How are you feeling?"

"Better, thanks. Not good, but better."

"Oh good."

"Hey, did you hear about Hershel?" Harmony whispered.

"No, what?" Maggie asked, and then thought better of it. "You know what? Don't tell me. If he wants me to know, he'll tell me."

"Fine," Harmony said, leaning back and looking dejected, "goody two shoes."

"No, it's not that, I swear. It's just, I honestly don't want to know."

"OK, whatever you say. So, I'm not sure what the rules are about being sick? Do I still have to be here?"

"I have no idea," Maggie answered. "Probably not."

"OK, see you later then," Harmony said, getting up. "I really don't feel good."

As she left, Maggie looked around, and the place still looked fairly empty, even though service would start in about five minutes. As Maggie watched the non-resident church members trickling in, she noticed a new face. At least, she thought she was new. The girl looked familiar, but Maggie couldn't quite place her. She couldn't help but stare, so of course the girl caught her. She smiled and waved a timid little wave, and Maggie waved back. *Of course!* The Rite Aid girl! Not the NyQuil narc from the night before, but the girl who had asked her about haircuts. Maggie waved her over to where she was sitting. The girl shyly accepted the invitation.

"Hey," Maggie said, standing to officially greet her. "It's great to see you! How are you?"

"Good," the girl said, sitting down. Maggie wanted to kick herself for not memorizing the girl's nametag the first time they'd met.

"I'm Maggie," she said, smiling.

"Rebecca," the girl said.

"Nice to meet you, again, Rebecca," Maggie said.

The worship team started to play, so Maggie almost couldn't hear Rebecca when she said, "I was wondering if I could get a haircut."

"Of course! Right after church, OK?" Rebecca nodded. Maggie wasn't sure if Rebecca had even meant to come to church, or if she had just accidentally walked in for a haircut during church time, but Maggie decided ultimately it didn't matter.

Pastor was sick, so Steve took over the preaching duties. This wasn't a good thing. Maggie found herself frustrated that she had actually gotten a guest to come to church, and then the sermon was long, pointless, and all about how smart Steve was. The longer the sermon got, the more uncomfortable Maggie became. She wondered if maybe they *should have* skipped the service and gone straight to the haircut.

But, after the sermon and an unfruitful altar call, someone on the worship team had the wisdom to only play one song to close things out. At the end, Rebecca looked unscathed.

"Do you want to have some lunch with me, or do you want to go straight to the haircut?"

"Lunch?" Rebecca asked, confused.

"Yep, we all eat downstairs together. It's pretty good."

"Ah, no, that's OK. Can we just do the haircut?"

"Absolutely, right this way," Maggie said, starting toward the door.

"Are you sure? I don't want to make you miss lunch."

"No, really!" Maggie laughed. "It's fine. I just pigged out at breakfast. I'm not even close to being hungry." Maggie led her to the bathroom, which, Maggie was thankful, was empty at the moment. "Do you want me to shampoo you, or just spray you with a squirt bottle?"

Rebecca looked around as though she was kind of creeped out. Truth be told, the bathroom was kind of a disaster. "Um, this is where you do it?"

"Yep, right here," Maggie said, patting the seat of the folding chair.

Rebecca looked disgusted, and Maggie wondered if she was going to leave, but she didn't. She just stood there, frozen.

"You want to have a seat?"

Rebecca sat, slowly.

"What kind of a haircut did you have in mind?" Maggie asked, as she started to run a brush through Rebecca's long hair.

"I just haven't had a haircut in a really long time, and I want my hair shorter, like maybe shoulder length? And I'd like some bangs. I just want it to look more exciting than it does. Right now it just hangs there, you know what I mean?"

"Yes, I do, and yes, I can do that."

Maggie got to work, and was almost done when Rebecca said, "Hey, can I ask you something?"

"You bet."

"Well, I was just wondering. Do you really buy into all this Jesus stuff? Or are you just putting up with it so you can live here?"

Maggie panicked a little, afraid she would say the wrong thing. "I totally buy into the Jesus stuff. It really is true."

Rebecca was quiet for a few minutes and then she said, "That preacher said something that really got to me."

Maggie pushed down the urge to tell Rebecca that Steve wasn't a preacher and certainly wasn't their pastor. "Oh yeah, what's that?"

"He said that Jesus never forgets anyone, that if Jesus knows you one day, then twenty years later, he still knows you."

"Yeah, I think that's about right."

"Well, it just made me think. When I was little, I went to church for a while, and I really believed back then. I mean, I was just a kid, I didn't know any better, right?" She laughed nervously. "But now I wonder if, if Jesus is real, if he remembers that, if he remembers when I was a kid."

"I assure you, he is real, and he does remember that." Maggie was done with the haircut, but she didn't want to end the conversation, so she kept playing with Rebecca's hair, feigning the occasional snip.

"Huh. Well, maybe I'll come to church sometime then."

"That would be awesome, but it's not really about going to church, you know."

"No?" Rebecca said, sounding a little scared.

"Yeah, it's not. It's just about knowing Jesus personally. You can do that just by talking to him, and by reading the Bible. He wants to know you, so if you try, he will make it happen. I never used to go to church … until I lived in one anyway."

Rebecca didn't say anything to that, and Maggie was worried she'd pushed too hard, so she said, "All done! Do you want to take a look in the mirror?"

Rebecca stood up and took two steps toward the mirror. Then her face lit up in a smile Maggie hadn't yet seen. "It looks awesome!" she declared, fluffing it with both her hands. "I love it! Thank you so much!"

"You're welcome."

"I really wish I had some money to pay you."

"No worries, honestly. I like doing it."

"OK, well," Rebecca said awkwardly, heading toward the door.

"Let me walk you out," Maggie interrupted. "I'll try to find you a Bible you can take with you. Also," she continued, as they headed out into the hallway, "come back anytime if you want me to trim those bangs. They'll probably be in your eyes in about two weeks."

"OK, thanks. I will do that."

They reached the church office, where Maggie was planning to beg for a Bible, but the door was locked. Maggie was frustrated then and found herself actually mad at Cari. *How dare she get sick?*

"Sorry, Rebecca. This is where I was going to get the Bible from, but it's locked. But you know what? Wait right here. I'll go get you mine. It's full of my notes, but you can borrow it. Hang on, don't move," she said, and turned and ran all the way back to her room.

She grabbed her Bible, turned it upside down to dump out all the bookmarks and scraps of paper she'd stored in there, and then ran back to the front door. But Rebecca was gone.

Chapter 39

Maggie woke up the next morning certain she had been hit by a large, fast-moving truck. Her whole body ached, but that pain was totally trumped by the pain in her head. Nevertheless, she had to get to Brewer by nine, so she grabbed her head, her finger, and her scissors and got in her Spark. The fresh air helped, but only a little.

She found the test site without too much trouble. She was more than a little intimidated by all the other women—and one man—in line at the door. It looked like a line at a modeling agency. They were all well-dressed, with amazing hair, perfect makeup, and she could tell from inside her car that they all smelled good too. She hadn't even showered that morning. After a brief coughing fit, she dragged herself to the end of the line.

They opened the doors soon after, and the line moved quickly. When Maggie got to the front of it, an older—but still perfectly polished—woman asked to see her ID. Maggie gave it to her, and the woman looked at Maggie suspiciously.

"Massachusetts?"

"Yes," Maggie said, not sure what else to say. She was really learning to hate that license.

"This test is for a Maine license."

"Yes, I know. I live in Maine. Sorry, I just haven't gotten my license changed yet."

"Oh, OK, well what's your address now?" she asked, grabbing a pen.

"Um, I don't really have one."

The woman's suspicion visibly grew. "Well, how long have you lived in Maine?"

"Um, about two months."

The woman sighed dramatically and pulled her reading glasses down to the tip of her nose, so she could peer over them accusingly. But she didn't say anything.

Maggie felt a scary lump forming in her throat as she whispered, "See, I live in a church. I'm homeless. But I intend to work in Maine, so I need a Maine license."

The woman leaned back suddenly, as if Maggie was contagious, which she probably was, but not in the way the woman thought. She nodded and handed Maggie's ID back to her and waved her inside. Maggie gratefully obliged.

She found an empty desk in the back and tried to sink into it. She could feel everyone staring at her, whether they actually were or not. As another coughing fit came over her, she found herself wishing for the rapture.

Despite the fact that her head was throbbing and she was sweating profusely, she found the written portion of the exam manageable. Much of it was common sense, some of it came back to her from school, and she only had to make educated guesses on a few questions. When she finished, she looked around, but it seemed everyone else was still working, so she went over her questions a second time, and then a third.

Finally, it was time for the practical part of the exam, and the nerves took back over. She set up her station quickly and plugged in her curling iron. She barely had everything disinfected when the proctor announced it was time for curling.

As she got to work, she lost herself in what she was doing, and the nerves abated. Before she knew it, it was haircut time. This too, went well, though at one point, she could feel a tester's eyes boring a hole in her back. Nevertheless, her mannequin looked stunning.

Perm time was a little scarier. She hadn't done this in a *long* time. As soon as she got started, her nose began to run like a fountain, and she had no choice but to wipe it on her shoulder. Her hands were far too busy. So was her brain. Some of her rods looked lumpy, and she started to panic, but kept going. She was the last one to step back from her mannequin and she did so without confidence.

After that, color was a piece of cake. But when the proctor announced it was time for chemical relaxing, Maggie found that she no longer even cared whether she passed. She just wanted it to be over. Her feet hurt. Her head hurt. Even her neck hurt from the troublesome task of holding her head up. She just wanted to drink some NyQuil and lie down for a week.

Thinking of Galen and knowing that he was actually praying for her success, probably that exact moment, kept her going and got her through the facial and the nail care. As she dug through her bag for nail care supplies, she found some paper towels, one of which she promptly ripped into tiny pieces and shoved into her nostrils. Not pretty, but it stopped the fountain, and she got that fake finger looking fantastic.

Driving home, she thought about pulling over for a nap, but she was motivated to see Galen.

"Hey!" Galen said, looking up from a manual. He came around the counter as if he was going to hug her, but she stopped him.

"Hey," she said, "don't get too close. I'm sicker than a dog."

He stopped. "How did it go? Are you OK?"

"No, I feel like I'm going to die. But I think the test went OK. I'm really not sure, but we'll know in two weeks."

"They don't tell you right away?"

"They would, but it would've cost another 25 bucks."

"Well, that's obnoxious. Anyway, I'm sure you did great. Do you want to go upstairs and lie down a while?"

Maggie sighed. "Nah, I think I'm just gonna go home and go to bed. But thanks. And thanks for getting me all those supplies. And thanks for praying for me. And thanks for well, just being you. I'd give you a big hug if I could, but I've got the plague."

Galen laughed, "OK then, well, come on over when you're feeling better."

She tried to smile. "OK, love you."

"Love you too. I'll keep praying."

Chapter 40

By the following Monday, most of the people at the church had been restored to health, or at least, as healthy as they were before. Which is why Maggie was so surprised when, as she was giving Amy an early morning trim, Harmony raced by them both and threw up in the first bathroom stall. Amy, half her hair still up in clips, promptly got up and left the bathroom. Maggie fought the urge to do the same. "You OK, Harm?"

She came out of the stall wiping her mouth on her sleeve and headed to the sink. "Yeah, I don't know what that was. It just came on so sudden. Must be something I ate."

Maggie wondered otherwise, but she just said, "OK."

But the next morning, when Harmony threw up again, Maggie knew that if she didn't say something, someone would.

"Harmony, can I talk to you?" Maggie asked, sliding into the seat across from her at breakfast.

"Yeah, what's up?"

"I don't mean to be nosey, but I care about you and I just want to help."

Harmony looked at her suspiciously then. "What?"

"Is there any chance that you might be pregnant?" Then she hurriedly added, "I'm not judging or anything. I just wonder if you're having morning sickness."

Harmony just stared at her. Maggie couldn't tell if she was considering the question or considering how to kill her. Maggie waited for an interminable ten seconds and was just about to say something else awkward when Harmony said, "Yeah, actually. I probably am pregnant."

And then she started to cry.

Maggie moved to the other side of the table and put her arm around her. "It's OK, Harmony. Really, it'll be OK."

Harmony stood up and stepped back from her, fury in her eyes. "How can you say that? Are you an idiot? Don't tell me that everything will be OK," she said in a mocking sweet voice. "I'm not the one with the perfect man on my arm. I'm homeless and broke. I can't even afford an abortion." She said the last part so loud that anyone nearby couldn't help but hear her. "Screw you, Maggie. Screw you and your perfect boyfriend and your perfect life and your perfect hair. I hate you." And she was off.

Maggie finished her breakfast without tasting it. She was working so hard at not crying herself, she didn't notice when Pastor sat down opposite her. "Good morning," he said, sounding more serious than usual.

"Morning," Maggie said without making eye contact.

"So I hear the word abortion is flying around. Is there anything I can do?"

"I don't know," Maggie said, putting down her fork. "I don't know what to do."

"Well, have you told G?" he asked.

Maggie started to say that Harmony probably wouldn't like that, but then she figured out that the rumor had probably been twisted. She looked at him, "Um, Pastor? I'm not the one who is pregnant."

"Oh!" Pastor declared, leaning back from the table as if to reset himself. "So, who is? Harmony?"

Maggie didn't say yes. But she didn't say no either.

He nodded. "OK, sorry for the confusion. I'll go talk to her."

Maggie nodded. And then, as he was walking away, Maggie called out, "Be careful!"

Harmony wouldn't speak to Maggie for several days after that. Maggie asked her how she was doing, how she was feeling, and told her she wanted to help, but Harmony wouldn't respond. At one point, Jackie said, "Just leave her alone, Maggie. Why do you even try?"

It wasn't spring yet, but Maggie was starting to feel some spring fever. The truth was, she was starting to tire of the shelter. It wasn't a horrible place to be, but she was starting to feel a bit smothered. She was never, ever alone, and she was beginning to feel desperate for some solitude. She started taking walks, but couldn't help but notice the dirty looks she got from other walkers, and even from people driving by. *Oh look, one of those homeless people out walking around, not working.*

When she finished the last book in the church library, which was unbearably bad, she walked to the Mattawooptock library. She figured some Stephen King would help.

"We don't give library cards to people in the shelter," the librarian exclaimed.

"What?" Maggie asked, dumbfounded.

"Well, they move around so much, in and out, we just decided that it wasn't wise to lend them books. We'd have no way of finding them if they decided to take off."

"Is that even legal?"

The librarian looked at Maggie as if she was a moron. "Yes, of course it's legal. The Mattawooptock library is for Mattawooptock residents, not vagrants."

Maggie sighed. "OK, well, can I just sit and read here, then?"

The librarian looked down at the counter. "I don't think that would be a good idea. Surely there must be books at the shelter?"

At Bible study that night, Pastor announced that they would be opening the addition the following Sunday. People cheered. "We'll be having a ceremony. Some of the people from the sponsoring church in Texas will be flying up to help us cut the ribbon. If it weren't for their generosity, we wouldn't even have this addition. So, thank you all for your patience. We'll soon be having much more room around here."

When Maggie got back to her room, Harmony was there alone. Before Maggie could say anything, Harmony said, "I've decided to keep the baby."

"Good, Harmony. That's great. Congratulations."

"That's a pretty stupid thing to say, Maggie."

Chapter 41

The next Monday, Maggie used Galen's internet connection to look up her test scores. They weren't there yet. She hung around his apartment, hitting the refresh button every twenty minutes or so until finally, there is was. Her 76. The equivalent of a D-. She shrieked and jumped for joy. She gave Eddie a celebratory squeeze and then went down to the garage to tell Galen.

He was just as excited as she was. He gave her a big, long hug and then held her away at arm's length and just stood there looking at her. "This calls for a celebration. What should we do? You name it."

"Thai food," she said without hesitating.

He laughed. "Way to go for something different. You go call it in, and I'll finish up here."

As they indulged in drunken noodles, Galen said, "Do you want to do anything for Valentine's Day? I mean, I know how much you enjoyed New Year's Eve."

She looked at him sharply, but his eyes were twinkly.

"No, I don't want to do anything for Valentine's Day. It's a stupid fake holiday, and you've already spent way too much money on me."

Galen nodded and said, "Deal."

So Maggie was surprised when he showed up at her door five days later on February 14, with Eddie in his arms. "Do you have a minute?" he asked.

"Of course!" she said, happy to see them both. She scooped Eddie into her arms and gave Galen a peck on the cheek. "Why is Eddie here?"

"Well," Galen said, sounding nervous and unsure of himself, "I wanted to show you something, and I thought Eddie should be here."

"OK," Maggie said, curious.

"Right this way, my dear." She and Eddie followed him toward the addition.

A brand new door stood between them and the addition, but it was shut, and there was plastic over it, making it quite clear that the door wasn't cleared for use.

Galen ripped back the plastic anyway.

"Galen!" Maggie gasped.

He smiled as if he was king of the jungle, and Maggie felt her heart tingle. "It's OK, I got permission from the boss."

Maggie wasn't sure whether he meant Pastor Dan, Cari, or God, but she followed him through the door. The addition looked less finished than she had expected, given people were going to be moving in the next day. Galen seemed to read her mind, "They'll be letting us do most of the finish work, but it's safe to move into for now. We can do carpet and paint anytime."

She looked around, amazed at how spacious it seemed. Galen stopped walking in front of a door that said "Salon."

"You ready?" he said, smiling at her.

He opened the door and reached inside to flick a switch. When he did, soft light flooded the shiny, very much finished room. Along the left-hand wall sat what looked like a brand new sofa, and it was *chic*. On the right side was a complete station, with a new salon chair, counter, and sink. Along the back, a dryer and chair, and a wall of shelves completely stocked with product.

Maggie couldn't breathe. She looked at him.

"Do you like it?"

"I don't understand. What is this?"

"No pressure," he said. "Pastor said you could use it as long as you want. You've shown us that it's important to have such a place here, so if you move on, we'll just pray God sends someone else to take over what you've started. But for now, this is your new salon. Do you like it?"

She still hadn't managed to breathe. "Do I *like* it? Galen, I don't know what to say. Thank you. Did you do this?"

He laughed. "Well, no. I had the idea, and I talked to Pastor. Then he talked to the contractors. I picked out all the furniture. I hope you like it. I almost asked you for your input a few times, but I really wanted to surprise you. And I spent a lot of time at the beauty supply store. They were a huge help. When we went there to get the mannequin, they already knew me well. I was afraid they would say something that would spill the beans, but they didn't. Phew!" he said, playfully wiping his brow.

"Yeah, phew is right," she said, walking into her new salon for the first time. She couldn't believe how beautiful it was, how clean, how spacious. Surrounding the chair was a squishy matt. She stepped onto it and then bounced up and down. It felt like Eden for her feet. There was a coffee table in front of the couch, and someone—she assumed Galen—had even put magazines on it. She grinned, imagining him buying *Cosmo* and *Oprah* at Hannaford.

Galen pointed to an empty frame over the station. "See that?"

She nodded.

"That's for your license."

Maggie started to cry.

"Are you OK? If you're up for it, I've got one more thing to show you."

She looked around, unable to imagine what else there could be. She just nodded.

"Great," he said, looking nervous again. He took her hand and led her to the salon chair. "Have a seat." She did. As he got down on one knee, she thought he meant to tie her shoe, but when she saw the ring box, she figured out what was really happening.

She gasped, again, and wondered if she would ever be able to breathe right again. Before he could even start speaking, she said, "Galen!"

"Margaret Hansen, I have loved you from the first moment I saw you. You have changed my life. You have made it wonderful. You have made it worth living. I can't imagine going back to a life without you, and I don't want to. You can keep living here if you want to, but I want you to be my wife. I want to be your husband. I want to try to love you the way Christ loves his church. I want to spend the rest of my life with you. Will you marry me?"

That was a lot of words for Galen, and she was impressed. He hadn't even brought a cue card. She leaned down and gave him a long kiss. "Of course I'll marry you. I love you. And I want to be your wife too." She leaned back in the chair and laughed. "And of course, it will be hard to move out of the homeless shelter, but I'm willing to do it—for you."

He laughed too. "Well, thank you. That means a lot." He took her hand and slid the ring onto her finger. It was a little snug, so he stopped, but she reached down and wiggled it the rest of the way on.

"It's beautiful. Thank you Galen," she said, and kissed him again. And as she did, she silently thanked her God, for bringing her home.

Epilogue

The addition opened a week behind schedule, which Pastor declared wasn't bad, all things considered. A vanload of Texans did arrive for the ribbon cutting, and there were reporters and photographers from Portland to Bangor. Pastor gave a moving speech, which of course, included the Gospel message, but most of that didn't make it into the newspaper articles or onto the screen.

Maggie opened her salon for business, and even though she could now legally charge people, she didn't. She did put out a new tip jar though, and she sometimes made enough to cover the cost of supplies. The church helped out with the rest.

The church also helped plan the wedding, which was, of course, held at the church. Everyone was invited. Maggie looked absolutely stunning. She found an amazing dress at a consignment store in Waterville. It fit as though it was tailored just for her. Harmony did Maggie's hair. While she worked, Jackie held onto a squirming baby boy. His name is Daniel.

CPSIA information can be obtained
at www.ICGtesting.com
Printed in the USA
LVOW10s2341271016
510641LV00007B/116/P